"Leon, I mean Noel!"

Mrs. Carillon shrieked and threw her arms around a skinny man with brown hair, red moustache, and sunglasses. The little man struggled desperately to free himself from her tight embrace.

She didn't realize her mistake until a pretty blonde woman hissed, "Seymour, what are you doing?" and yanked him out of her arms. Mrs. Carillon watched the couple hasten away. She was too confused and embarrassed to feel someone tapping her on the shoulder.

"Mrs. Carillon?" And another tap.

Mrs. Carillon spun around. A tall, clean-shaven man with brown hair and sunglasses smiled down at her.

"Leon?" she asked in a hoarse whisper.

"Noel," he replied.

NOVELS BY ELLEN RASKIN

The Mysterious Disappearance of Leon (I mean Noel)
Figgs & Phantoms
The Tattooed Potato and other clues
The Westing Game

Ellen Raskin

THE MYSTERIOUS DISAPPEARANCE OF LEON (I MEAN NOEL)

PUFFIN BOOKS
An Imprint of Penguin Group (USA) Inc.

PUFFIN BOOKS

Published by the Penguin Group

Penguin Young Readers Group, 345 Hudson Street, New York, New York 10014, U.S.A.
Penguin Group (Canada), 90 Eglinton Avenue East, Suite 700, Toronto, Ontario, Canada M4P 2Y3
(a division of Pearson Penguin Canada Inc.)
Penguin Books Ltd, 80 Strand, London WC2R 0RL, England
Penguin Ireland, 25 St Stephen's Green, Dublin 2, Ireland (a division of Penguin Books Ltd)
Penguin Group (Australia), 250 Camberwell Road, Camberwell, Victoria 3124, Australia
(a division of Pearson Australia Group Pty Ltd)
Penguin Books India Pvt Ltd, 11 Community Centre, Panchsheel Park, New Delhi - 110 017, India
Penguin Group (NZ), 67 Apollo Drive, Rosedale, North Shore 0632, New Zealand
(a division of Pearson New Zealand Ltd)
Penguin Books (South Africa) (Pty) Ltd, 24 Sturdee Avenue,
Rosebank, Johannesburg 2196, South Africa

Registered Offices: Penguin Books Ltd, 80 Strand, London WC2R 0RL, England

First published in the United States of America by E. P. Dutton,
a division of NAL Penguin Inc., 1971
Published by Puffin Books, 1989.
This edition published simultaneously by Puffin Books and Dutton Children's Books,
divisions of Penguin Young Readers Group, 2011

1 3 5 7 9 10 8 6 4 2

Text and illustrations © Ellen Raskin, 1971
All rights reserved

THE LIBRARY OF CONGRESS HAS CATALOGED THE PUFFIN EDITION AS FOLLOWS:
Raskin, Ellen
The mysterious disappearance of Leon (I mean Noel)
Reprint. Originally published: New York : Dutton, c. 1971.
Summary: The disappearance of her husband is only the first
of the mysteries Mrs. Carillon must solve.
ISBN 0-14-032945-5
[1. Mystery and detective stories. 2. Humorous stories.] I. Title.
Pz7.R1817My 1989   —[Fic]   88-30658

Puffin ISBN 978-0-14-241700-3

Printed in the United States of America
Set in Times Roman

This book is dedicated to Claire Laporte,
a reader who has grown up with my picture books.

Contents

Names

It's a funny thing about names. Some are long, some are short; some mean something, others don't; but everyone and everything has one, or two or three.

Little Dumpling Fish had four names. Her first name was Caroline. Her nickname was Little Dumpling. Her last name was Fish, but that was changed to Carillon* when she married Leon Carillon—all because of a pot of soup.

As for Leon, he changed his name to ? .

A Pot of Soup

Mr. and Mrs. Fish and five-year-old Little Dumpling lived on a small farm next to the small farm of Mr. and Mrs. Carillon and their skinny son Leon. The Fishes grew tomatoes; the Carillons grew potatoes.

Thanksgiving used to be a happy time when the two families sat down together to a twelve-course turkey dinner. This November, snow was already on the ground, firewood was in short supply, and there was no money for either turkey or trimmings. What kind of a feast could they make out of tomatoes and potatoes?

* Pronounced like "carry on" with an "l" in between.

3.

"Soup," decided Mrs. Fish.

Mrs. Fish arrived at the Carillon kitchen early in the morning, determined to make the best soup anyone had ever tasted. The two wives grated potatoes, pulped tomatoes, chopped parsley, and diced onions. What they did next is still a closely guarded secret,* but they fussed over the simmering pot all day long.

****

The table looked almost festive. Steam rising from the soup bowls masked the chips in the Carillons' china, and a candle stub flickered from its saucer over the purple-flowered tablecloth.

Mr. Fish was the first to sip the soup. The cooks stared, waiting for his opinion. Mr. Fish stared back. Mr. Fish's eyes bulged.

"Yipes!" he cried, and spit the soup halfway across the table, dousing the candle. The children giggled; the women were horrified. "Too hot," he said, fanning his red tongue.

"Blow!" said Mrs. Fish, and everyone blew.

Mr. Carillon was the next to sip the soup.

"Slurp," he said, and blew and slurped again.

"Wonderful," Mr. Carillon announced at last. "Wonderful soup."

Leon, imitating his father, blew and slurped. "Wonderful," he said. "Wonderful soup."

Mr. Fish tried again. "Good is good, and this soup is good," he said and took another mouthful. "It's better than good."

* People have said they added dried ragweed ever since Albert I. Gluck set a new record of 7,794 consecutive sneezes ten minutes after eating a bowl of this soup.

Another mouthful. "Best soup I've ever tasted."

Everyone was eating heartily now; everyone but Little Dumpling Fish, who wasn't taking any chances. She was still blowing.

Two helpings, three helpings, four for Mr. Fish, and the pot was empty. For the first time, in a long time, their stomachs were full.

The Naming of the Soup

Leon and Little Dumpling were building a snowman in the backyard. Their mothers were scrubbing pots. The men were still sitting at the table, still praising the soup.

"Best soup I've ever tasted," Mr. Fish said for the tenth time.

"Best soup *anybody's* ever tasted." Mr. Carillon said.

"Hmmm," hmmed Mr. Fish, fishing for something new to say. "We should put it on the market, it's so good."

"Probably make us a million dollars," said Mr. Carillon, wanting the last word.

"A million dollars!" shouted Mrs. Fish, running in from the kitchen with Mrs. Carillon close on her heels. ·

"Money is money," * especially when you don't have any; and these two families were so poor that the women had to patch ᴜᴉe patches on their threadbare clothes. "A million dollars!" she repeated.

"Let's see," Mrs. Carillon said, "to begin with, we'd need three more pots and a bigger chopping block. . ."

"And Ball jars and sealing wax. . ."

"And labels."

* One of Mr. Fish's favorite expressions, along with "Boys will be boys."

"Bet we could put up five hundred pints a month, easy," said Mrs. Fish.

"You might just have something there," Mr. Carillon said, impressed with her instant arithmetic.

Mr. Fish nodded in agreement.

"We'll start small," he predicted, "but in no time, mark my word, we'll make that million dollars. Half for you, and half for us."

"Half?" shouted Mr. Carillon. "What do you mean, half? The soup was made in *my* house in *my* pot on *my* stove with *my* potatoes."

"The soup was *my* idea," Mrs. Fish insisted.

"And those were *my* tomatoes," shouted Mr. Fish. "Besides, fair is fair."

Mr. Carillon folded his arms and stared defiantly at his neighbors. "This is *my* house, and besides, I've already named the soup. Carillon's Pomato Soup."

"What?" screamed Mr. Fish, jumping up and knocking over his chair.

"You heard me. Carillon's Pomato Soup."

"Fish's Pomato Soup!"

"Carillon's Pomato Soup!"

"Fish's Pomato Soup!" Mr. Fish pounded his fist on the table. The dishes clanked; the candle fell; a soup spoon flew through the air, smack into Mr. Carillon's eye.

****

Leon and Little Dumpling peered through the window. Their mittens were soaked and their toes were numb with cold, but they thought it best to stay where they were.

"My father's going to beat up your father," Leon said, trying to start a fight of his own to keep warm; but Little

Dumpling Fish plopped down on a snow pile and cried.* Leon had to stand on his head to cheer her up.

****

"It all boils down to two problems," Mrs. Fish explained after she had convinced the men to sit down and talk it over, "the sharing of the profits, and the naming of the soup."

They argued and argued until the Fishes convinced the Carillons that fifty-fifty was fair and proper.

Naming the soup was another matter. The Fishes agreed that neither "Fish and Carillon's Pomato Soup" nor "Carillon and Fish's Pomato Soup" sounded very appetizing; but they refused to call the soup "Carillon's." The Carillons refused to call it anything else.

Night was falling and they were no nearer a solution than when they began. Suddenly Mrs. Fish noticed the darkened window. "The children!" she cried, hastening to the door.

"That's it!" Mr. Carillon shouted. "The children!" He waited until he had everyone's attention. "We'd have no problem with the name of the soup if both children had the name of Carillon."

Mrs. Fish was horrified. "You want to adopt Little Dumpling? Never!"

"No, no," Mr. Carillon said, "what I mean is that your daughter must marry my son."

The Fishes thought if over.

"What if they grow up and don't want to marry each other?" said Mr. Fish. "What if Little Dumpling grows

---

* Little Dumpling had little to fear. Her father was a foot taller and fifty pounds heavier than Mr. Carillon.

up and marries Augie Kunkel down the road? You've still got your name on our soup."

The Carillons thought it over.

There was only one solution: Leon and Little Dumpling must be married right away. No tomato could be chopped or one potato peeled until the wedding had taken place.

"After all," Mr. Fish said, "business is business."

Two Mrs. Carillons

Two weeks later, when their runny noses had slowed to trickles, five-year-old Little Dumpling Fish and seven-year-old Leon Carillon stood before the preacher in the Fishes' cold living room. Everyone was shivering in his thin Sunday-best except the bride, who wore boots under the long purple-flowered dress made out of the Carillons' tablecloth.

"Do you, Caroline Fish, take this man for your law-ful-wedded husband. . . ?"

Little Dumpling giggled.

"Do you, Leon Carillon, take this woman for your lawful-wedded wife. . . ?"

Leon sneezed.

Either the preacher accepted a giggle and a sneeze as answers, or he couldn't hear through his earmuffs. He pronounced the children "man and wife."

Whereupon Mr. Fish made a speech.

"Fun is fun, but now it's time to get down to business. From this moment on, so there's no mistaking the fact that the Fishes own half of Carillon's Pomato Soup, my daughter shall be called by one and all, and that includes

everybody, including Leon: Caroline Caroline. . . !
I mean Carillon Carillon. . . ! I mean. . . ."

Mr. Fish curled his lips and twisted his tongue, but
Caroline Carillon just wouldn't come out.

Mrs. Fish suggested Little Dumpling Carillon, but Little Dumpling hated her nickname and Mr. Fish said it
wasn't dignified enough for a soup heiress.

"From this moment on," Mr. Fish announced, "everybody, including Leon, calls my daughter Mrs. Carillon!"

"But I'm Mrs. Carillon," protested Leon's mother.

Mr. Fish shouted, "A bargain is a bargain," and there
was even talk of a divorce; but the argument was finally
settled. Leon's mother would be called "Mrs. Carillon,"
Little Dumpling would be called "Mrs. Carillon," and
the soup would be called "*Mrs.* Carillon's Pomato Soup."

Business Booms. Boom! *

Mrs. Carillon's Pomato Soup was an instant success. Pov-
erty had spread throughout the land, and poor people
found they could feed a family on a ten-cent can of the
rich soup. Mr. Fish and Mr. Carillon brought in more or-
ders than their wives could fill. Cooks and canners were
hired, and a factory was built spanning both farms. In no
time at all the Fishes and the Carillons became one mil-
lionaire each.

The two families decided to keep the children apart
until Leon was twenty-one. Leon was sent away to the
Seymour Hall Boarding School for Boys, where he lived
summer and winter. He never returned for holidays or
vacations, not even for the funeral.

* Somewhere in this section is the clue to   ?

No respectable girls' school would accept a married woman, so little Mrs. Carillon had to be educated at home. Mrs. Fish hired the first governess to apply for the job, mean Miss Anna Oglethorpe.

What Miss Anna Oglethorpe lacked in imagination and kindness, she made up for in bones: big, knobby shoulder bones, elbow bones, knee bones; long, thin hand bones and even longer foot bones; and a large, sharp, twice-hooked nose bone. One or more of these bones always seemed to be aimed at Mrs. Carillon—jutting, poking, slapping, kicking—especially when she was caught daydreaming. Miss Anna Oglethorpe hated dreamers (she never had a dream in her entire life), and Mrs. Carillon had little to do but dream.

She seldom saw her parents anymore. They were too busy running the business during the day and counting their money at night. She never saw Leon. Sometimes Mr. Kunkel, the factory foreman, brought his motherless son Augie to the Fishes' big, new house during school holidays. Augie Kunkel was her one playmate and her only friend; then he, too, was sent away.

Mrs. Carillon would never forget the day Augie was sent to live with his aunt. It was the day that she became an orphan and the only Mrs. Carillon. It was her twelfth birthday.

****

Miss Anna Oglethorpe had caught her nose between the swinging pantry doors and was upstairs in bed, her face buried under ice packs.

"Happy Birthday to me," twelve-year-old Mrs. Carillon muttered, chin in hand, alone at the breakfast table. Her parents had forgotten her birthday. They had dashed out of the house hours ago to attend a directors' meeting at the factory.

The meeting was well under way when Mrs. Fish accused Mr. Carillon of out-and-out theft, or was it the other way around? No matter, for just as Mr. Fish pounded the table and shouted "Fair is fair," the boiler on the floor below blew up.

The explosion was heard five miles away. By the time the fire was put out, one wing of the factory had been gutted. The rubble was cleared and sifted; but no identifiable remains of the Fishes, the Carillons, Mr. Kunkel, or the sales manager were ever found.

People began to wonder about the missing bodies. People began to say the soup tasted a bit peculiar after that.

Luckily a Mr. Banks, trustee of the estate, was able to save the business from total ruin. He eased the minds of the suspicious soupeaters with a clever jingle he wrote to the tune of "On Wisconsin." It was sung by a hundred-man chorus over every radio station in the country, twenty-five times a day for a year.

> *In Pomato, in Pomato,*
> *You will find no meat;*
> *Mrs. Carillon's Pomato,*
> *Soup that can't be beat.*
> *U-rah-rah!*
> *Our Pomato, our Pomato,*
> *Just ten cents a can,*
> *Is the soup, the soup, soup, soup*
> *That's ve-ge-tar-i-an.*

Black and Blue and Purple

It wasn't the explosion that frightened Mrs. Carillon; it was Miss Anna Oglethorpe screaming, "Armageddon!" *
Both thought of hiding in the window seat, but the twelve-year-old got there first. The frantic governess clomped down the stairs at top speed, lifted the seat, and too flustered to see it was already occupied, began to climb in. All Mrs. Carillon could do to protect herself was sink her teeth into a big, knobby ankle bone.

Miss Anna Oglethorpe let out a piercing shriek. She hopped about in dizzying circles, then dashed through the hallway and dived into the narrow laundry chute.

Every bone in her body hit one part or another of the tin lining during her headlong fall. Thunderous reverberations boomed up and down the shaft, and in and out of her skull. She landed on a pile of dirty linens and lay, sore and trembling, entangled in soiled socks and sheets for two days, her brains addled, temporarily deafened. A wet bath towel, thrown from the second floor, finally brought her to her senses.

Miss Anna Oglethorpe's bruises disappeared within a

* The battle between good and evil when the world comes to an end. Miss Anna Oglethorpe obviously thought that the "good guys" were winning.

week; but Mrs. Carillon, world's champion daydreamer, remained black and blue for the next seven years.

****

At times she thought those seven long years of pokes and jabs and smells of simmering soups would never end; then suddenly, one day, her dream came true.

Leon's fourteenth card with the fourteenth message had arrived.

****

Nineteen-year-old Mrs. Carillon locked the last suitcase and studied herself once more in the full-length mirror. She was singing one of Leon's messages at the top of her lungs, because she was happy, and because it hurt Miss Anna Oglethorpe's sensitive ears.

"Grown a moustache—it's red, red, red. . . ." *

Every December 9th Leon had written her a message inside identical wedding anniversary cards decorated with violets. Mrs. Carillon knew every word of the fourteen messages by heart; still, she wondered what her husband looked like as a grown man. Would she recognize him?

"No problem," she thought as she pinned a stray black curl in place. "Leon, I mean Noel, is sure to recognize me." She appeared taller than her five feet in her purple high-heeled shoes; but she had to admit that she still looked something like a dumpling. Besides, she was wearing a purple-flowered dress. . . .

A car horn honked. Mr. Banks had arrived to drive her to the station.

---

* Message 12. Strange, for Leon had brown hair, but not impossible.

Mrs. Carillon grabbed her bags stuffed with purple-flowered resort clothes and ran down the stairs.

"Good-by soup! Good-by house!" she shouted.

"And good-by, forever, Miss Anna Oglethorpe!"

Leon's Fourteen Messages*

1. Hi! *Leon*
2. I am fine. How are you? *Leon*
3. I hate school. I'm the smallest one here. *Leon.*
4. Got to wear glasses because I can't see the blackboard. *Leon.*
5. My best friend is called Pinky. *Leon*
6. I'm writing the story of my life. You are in it. *Leon*
7. I'm going to wear a black tie to mourn my folks from now on and always. *Leon*
8. Who wrote that awful soup song? I can't stand it! I hate the song as much as I hate the soup. In fact, I hate all soup—except won ton. *Leon* (I hate my name, too!)
9. Pinky taught me how to ride a horse—it's great fun, except the stable only has slow nags. I think I'll get a horse of my own. *Noel* (That's my new name. It's much more genteel, don't you think?)
10. Help! Mr. Banks won't let me buy a horse. Try and make him change his mind. *Noel*
11. Found a great job. Tell tight-wad Banks to keep his old riding boots—I don't need handouts. *Noel*
12. Grown a moustache. It's red! *Noel*

---

* Some very important clues here. You don't have to memorize all the messages as Mrs. Carillon did; a bookmark will do.

13. Shaved off my moustache. *Noel*
14. Meet me at the Seaside Hotel, Palm Beach, this Friday. *Noel*

Leon? Noel!

No one in the lobby of the Seaside Hotel recognized her, or her purple-flowered dress. She announced herself to the desk clerk and was handed a key to room 1164. No one was in the room.

Mrs. Carillon wondered whether today was Friday; then she saw the note in the familiar handwriting propped up on the desk.

> *Put on a bathing suit and meet me at the dock.*
> *Noel*

No one seemed to recognize her, or her purple-flowered swimsuit. She jostled through the throng of vacationers looking for—no, not a black tie, no one wore neckties with bathing trunks—glasses, perhaps, and a red. . . . Suddenly, she saw him.

"Leon, I mean Noel!" Mrs. Carillon shrieked and threw her arms around a skinny man with brown hair, red moustache, and sunglasses. The little man struggled desperately to free himself from her tight embrace.

She didn't realize her mistake until a pretty blonde woman hissed, "Seymour, what are you doing?" and yanked him out of her arms. Mrs. Carillon watched the couple hasten away. She was too confused and embarrassed to feel someone tapping her on the shoulder.

"Mrs. Carillon?" And another tap.

Mrs. Carillon spun around. A tall, clean-shaven man with brown hair and sunglasses smiled down at her.

"Leon?" she asked in a hoarse whisper.

"Noel," he replied.

*The Last Message**

It was an awkward moment, not at all the way she had dreamed it would be. Fourteen years had passed; they had grown up into strangers.

"We still have time for a sail," Noel said at last. "Let's go!"

Mrs. Carillon studied her handsome husband as he guided the sailboat out of the bay. "I never would have recognized you," she said.

Noel turned to her and smiled.

She smiled.

They sat there and smiled.

They didn't move; the boat didn't move. It hung suspended on the crest of a monstrous wave. It teetered. It crashed into the thrashing sea, smashed.

Mrs. Carillon somersaulted into the wild water, rose to the surface, climbed onto the broken hull, and looked about her.

"Leon, Leon!" she shouted at the bobbing head a few yards away. The head went under; the head came up; the head went under; the head came up.

"Leon!" she cried.

And he answered:

"Noel *glub* C *blub* all. . .I *glub* new. . . ." †

****

* Hereupon referred to as the *glub-blubs*.
† That's it! Copy it down, or memorize it; most of all, try to solve it.

Mrs. Carillon didn't know what hit her, or what happened next. Two days later she woke up in a hospital with an aching head.

"How's Leon—Noel?" were her first words.

"Leon Noel?" repeated the nurse. "You must mean the man who was rescued with you. Just a cut on the elbow. We patched him up right away and let him go."

Mrs. Carillon returned to the hotel, but Noel was no longer registered there. The only message was a checkroom stub for her luggage. She finally found a bellhop who remembered delivering a plane ticket to a man of her description.

"A ticket to New York, I think."

A Pain in the Arm

Cafifi, Carigan, Carillon Furs, Carillon Records, Carin . . . No Noel Carillon was listed in the New York City telephone book, and "Information" never heard of him.

Mrs. Carillon phoned the furriers. No one there knew anyone named Carillon; no one could even remember how the company got its name.

She phoned the record store. The owner, a Mr. Spitz, said he had chosen the name "Carillon" because it sounded so musical.

She phoned Mr. Banks. No, he had no idea where Noel could be. Why doesn't she come back home and wait for him there?

Back to bony Miss Anna Oglethorpe? Never!

Mrs. Carillon didn't know what to do next. Confused and frightened, she knelt in the airport phone booth and prayed that Noel would come for her.

Noel didn't come.

She prayed and prayed some more, and still Noel didn't come.

Then she remembered what her father always said: "Nobody gets nothing for nothing." She would give anything to find Noel; but what did she have to give?

She would give her half of the Pomato Soup fortune to charity, if only Noel would come for her. Her ten-room house. Her purple-flowered clothes. Her dimples. Her right arm . . . and then the phone rang.

She jumped up and a hot, searing pain shot through her right arm. "Leon, Noel?" she shouted into the mouthpiece.

"Hello, Max's Delicatessen?

"Two corned beef sandwiches, lean, and don't forget the pickles," said the dangling receiver as Mrs. Carillon hobbled, stiff-kneed, away from the phone booth. Tears streamed down her cheeks and nose and off her chin; but her right arm didn't hurt anymore.

A Letter to Mr. Banks

Dear Mr. Banks:

Here I am, still in New York City. I am not coming home. I have made up my mind that the important thing is to find Noel. You see, I have a feeling that he is suffering from amnesia, or even worse. Whatever the trouble is, I just know he needs me; and I need him very much.

Please let me know if you hear from him—right away!

You will notice the hotel's name and address on this stationery. This is where to send me some money to get by on. Don't pay any attention to the telephone number.* I will be in and out of my room so much that I won't be here when you call.

A very Merry Christmas to you,
Mrs. Carillon

---

* Mrs. Carillon never again used the telephone after "don't forget the pickles."

25.

*Bulletin Sent to the Bureau of Missing Persons,
the F.B.I., and the U.S. Post Office*

MISSING

Noel Carillon, alias Leon Carillon

Age: 21
Height: About 6'2". Weight: Thin. Eyes: Nearsighted.
Sometimes has red moustache; always has brown hair.
Wears black neckties except with bathing trunks.
Handsome. Genteel. Can stand on his head.
Likes horses and won ton soup.
(Owns half of a soup. Does not own a horse.)
May be in company of man called Pinky.
Occupation: Yes.

The Meaning of the Glub-blubs

Message:
Noel *glub* C *blub* all. . .I *glub* new. . . .

1. Noel = Noel. (I must have called him "Leon.")
2. C *blub* all. . . .
    ball
    call
    fall
    gall
    hall—(a good possibility! City Hall?)
    mall
    Paul—(St. Paul's?)
    shawl
    tall
    wall
3. I *glub* new. . . . = in New York City

Solution:
Noel. City Hall (or St. Paul's) in New York City*

* It took Mrs. Carillon two weeks to figure out this solution, and two
  words are absolutely correct. Now, if it had taken her eight
  weeks. . .

Mrs. Carillon's Plan of Search

1. CITY HALL: Watch the people who work there and about. Check voting lists; licenses (drivers' and dog).

2. ST. PAUL'S: Six churches in New York City with that name, including Baptist, Methodist, Lutheran, and Roman Catholic. Try one each Sunday.

3. WON TON SOUP: Eat in Chinese restaurants only. (List of 78 names and addresses attached.)

4. HORSES: Read *Racing Form* and *The Morning Telegraph* every day. Make special note of horse buyers. Also, see all new cowboy movies.

5. STORY OF MY LIFE: Ask librarian for autobiographies of writers using pen names.

6. ALSO: Send missing person bulletin to all hotels, opticians, optometrists, ophthalmologists, and riding stables in New York City.

7. JUST IN CASE: Wear purple-flowered clothes.

Another Letter to Mr. Banks

Dear Mr. Banks:

Sorry about those doctors' bills. I had to go through all sorts of tests, but you will be happy to hear it was nothing serious—just an allergic reaction* to too much soy sauce.

You're right, it's nearly a year since I began my search; but I can't agree with you, Mr. Banks, when you say that Noel must be dead or he'd have asked for money by now. I still think my idea of amnesia is closer to the truth. And the reason I haven't found him is this: Noel is *not* in New York City. He just isn't the type of person to live here (even if he doesn't know who he is)—it's much too big and lonely.

So, you see, I am not about to come home. I am going to New Brockton, Alabama, instead.

May I wish you and yours a happy Thanksgiving,
Mrs. Carillon

* Hives.

Possible Solutions of "New. . . ." *

Noel. City Hall (or St. Paul's) in:

New Brockton, Alabama
Nutrioso, Arizona
Newport, Arkansas
Newport Beach, California
New Raymer, Colorado
New Britain, Connecticut
New Haven, Connecticut
New London, Connecticut
Newark, Delaware
Newberry, Florida
Newington, Georgia
New Meadows, Idaho
New Lenox, Illinois
New Albany, Indiana
New Hampton, Iowa
New Cambria, Kansas
Newport, Kentucky
New Iberia, Louisiana
New Orleans, Louisiana
New Vineyard, Maine
New London, Maryland
New Market, Maryland
Newton, Massachusetts
New Buffalo, Michigan
New Ulm, Minnesota
Newhebron, Mississippi
New Franklin, Missouri

Newman Grove, Nebraska
New Year Lake, Nevada
Newport, New Hampshire
Newark, New Jersey
New Brunswick, New Jersey
Newkirk, New Mexico
Newburgh, New York
New Rochelle, New York
Newton, North Carolina
New Leipzig, North Dakota
Newark, Ohio
Newkirk, Oklahoma
New Bridge, Oregon
New Castle, Pennsylvania
Newport, Rhode Island
Newry, South Carolina
New Underwood, South Dakota
New Tazewell, Tennessee
Newgulf, Texas
New Harmony, Utah
Newfane, Vermont
Newport News, Virginia
Newport, Washington
Newburg, West Virginia
New Glarus, Wisconsin
New Holstein, Wisconsin
New Haven, Wyoming †

* A correct word appears twice in this list.
† Only 47 states here. Alaska and Hawaii were not states when Mrs.
Carillon made this list, but one is still missing.

4 * Missing: One Husband.
Found: Two Twins

Twenty Years Later

"菜肴非常好," Mrs. Carillon said as she left the restaurant, fortune cookie in hand. She had learned to speak some Chinese over the past twenty years, had become an expert on city halls, St. Pauls', race horses, autobiographies, cowboy movies, and the geography of the United States; but she still had not found Noel.*

The people of Newport News stared as she strolled down the street, an image out of an old movie. No one but Mrs. Carillon wore curls piled high on top of the head, or long, flowered dresses, or teetering high heels. Even purple was out of style.

Mrs. Carillon sat down on a bench opposite City Hall, carefully broke open the cookie, and extracted the narrow strip of paper.

Many search, but few know what they seek.

She was so intent on reading her fortune that she didn't notice the dark-haired twins standing before her.

"Weren't you bitten by a werewolf on the early show

* The only Carillon she found was a registered Republican in New Iberia, Louisiana: Carillon, Casper. He was a seventy-five-year-old undertaker and no relation.

yesterday?" the boy asked. Mrs. Carillon was so startled she almost fell off the bench.

"I'm Tony and this is my sister Tina. You are a movie star, aren't you?"

"No, I'm just Mrs. Carillon."

"Like the soup?" Tina asked.

Mrs. Carillon nodded.

"That's about all we ever have to eat at that miserable orphanage, Mrs. Carillon's miserable Pomato Soup."

"It makes me sneeze," Tony added.

"If you have a soup named after you, you must be rich and famous," Tina guessed.

"I'd rather have an ice cream named after me," said Tony.

"I had no choice," replied Mrs. Carillon, delighted to be talking to someone other than waiters and hotel clerks. "Besides, I'm not at all famous, just rich. And I'm an orphan, too."

Tina felt little sympathy for a rich, grown-up orphan. "We're twin orphans, which is worse, because we've each lost a mother and father. And nobody wants to adopt two children at once, especially eleven-year-olds going on twelve."

"You poor things!" Mrs. Carillon was deeply moved.

To Tina things were either miserable or getting worse, especially when she found a sympathetic ear.

"Even more miserable, next year they separate the boys from the girls and we won't even have each other."

This unhappy news was more than Mrs. Carillon could bear. She uttered a loud sob, and twenty years of tears flooded forth. The people of Newport News stared even harder.

"We'd better go find our class," Tony said, taking his sister by the hand.

"Don't go," cried Mrs. Carillon. "Don't ever go!"

The Traveling Carillons

"Next stop: Newport, Washington," announced Mrs. Carillon, who was now not only looking for her husband, but the father of her children. She had had no trouble adopting the twins once she had persuaded Mr. Banks to give the orphanage a large donation.

Tina and Tony were delighted with their funny new mother and her promises of cowboy movies and eating in Chinese restaurants across the United States. They couldn't wait to join in the search for Noel and solve the mystery of the missing husband.

They searched and searched. Tina's assignment: black ties; Tony's: red moustaches; Mrs. Carillon's: glasses.

"Next stop: Newburg, West Virginia," she announced two months later. And six weeks after that: "Next stop: New Glarus, Wisconsin." Then: "Next stop: New Holstein, Wisconsin."

****

"I've been thinking about 'I *glub* new. . . ,' " Mrs. Carillon said in New Haven, Wyoming, the last stop on her list. "And what I've decided is that '*glub*' must be a city and 'new' the state:

"City Hall (or St. Paul's) in *glub* New Hampshire."

Concord, New Hampshire; *Manchester, Nashua,** *Portsmouth* . . . the routine was always the same. Mrs.

---

* Also the name of a famous race horse.

Carillon rented a hotel suite, enrolled the twins in public school, and haunted the corridors of City Hall. Together they searched through seas of faces: on the street, on television, in buses and trains and cowboy films. Most towns didn't have a St. Paul's; several didn't have a Chinese restaurant; and none of them had a Noel Carillon.

Wrong!

It was Thursday, and Mrs. Carillon would be late. According to routine she would spend the afternoon in the beauty parlor having her graying hair dyed black, then stop off at the library before returning to the hotel.

"Routines are miserable, Chinese food is miserable, and hotel rooms are even worse," Tina complained.

They were in Albuquerque, New Mexico; at least the twins thought it was Albuquerque. All cities were beginning to look alike to them, all the train stations, all the hotels, and all the people. Even their classmates looked alike, for Tina and Tony never stayed in one school long enough to make friends.

"You know, Tony, sometimes I wonder just who, and what, I am. So I look at you to see who, and what, *you* are. And you know what I see?"

"What?"

"Nothing. Just a miserable orphan. We're still orphans, Tony, except now we're traveling orphans."

"Don't worry, once we find Noel. . . ."

"Sometimes I think we'll never find Noel. Sometimes I think that when we're in New Mexico, he's in New Hampshire; and when we're in New Hampshire, he's in New Jersey. And sometimes I think Mrs. Carillon isn't very smart."

"She's smarter than you," Tony said. "Since when do you know anything about horses—or speak Chinese?"

"If her Chinese is so good how come she broke out in hives again?"

"Maybe it's chicken pox." *

"Well, I still think we're smarter, especially since we're two and she's only one. And you know what else?"

Tony was too busy examining his arm for red bumps to answer.

"I think she's wrong about city hall and St. Paul's. And she's wrong about the 'New' states, too."

"Wrong?" It had never occurred to Tony that Mrs. Carillon might be wrong.

"That's right, wrong!" Tina repeated. "What's more, I think we can find a better solution. All we have to do is decide what we want, then get the *glub-blubs* to fit."

"What's that got to do with finding Noel?"

"Nothing, but we're not finding him this way, either," Tina replied. "As Mrs. Carillon always says: 'Many search, but few know what they seek.'"

"She also says: 'He who seeketh findeth,'" Tony said.

"Well, *I* know what *I* seeketh!"

Glub-blubs

"All right, so maybe I don't know what I seeketh," Tina admitted. An hour had passed and her paper headed "What I Want to Do and Where" was still blank. The only thing she could think of was what she *didn't* want to do: she didn't want to travel any more.

---

* Wrong! Mrs. Carillon said, "No soy sauce" in the Mandarin dialect, and the waiter only understood Fukien.

Tony had been working on the *glub-blubs* for some time. He handed Tina his list of ideas:

    C *blub* all = See carnivals
                    See the animal
                    See cannibals

Tina shook her head. "Mrs. Carillon will insist on: 'See carnival in New Brockton, Alabama; see carnival in Nutrioso, Arizona'; and we'd be traveling alphabetically again."

"How about 'See the animal. . .' "

"Same miserable problem."

"Let me finish!" Tony insisted. "See the animal in the New York Zoo!"

"New York Zoo?" Tina had to think that one over. She loved zoos, and Noel did like animals—horses, anyway; but they could never convince Mrs. Carillon to return to New York City.

Tony was more concerned with convincing his sister. "We'd have to stay a long, long time in New York City. It would take us years to face-watch eight million people."

"Four million," Tina argued. "We don't have to look at women. Or children, either, so that makes two million."

"All right, so two million," Tony agreed, knowing that he had made his point.

Tina had to admit that two million men meant years of searching; but she couldn't believe Mrs. Carillon would return to New York City just to "See the animal." What animal? Tina studied the *glub-blubs* once more.

Noel *glub* C *blub* all. . .I *glub* new. . . .

"Tony," she said excitedly. "What if Noel went under water in the middle of a word? What if he went under in the middle of 'C—all'?"

"C—all?" repeated Tony. "See-all, see-all? SEAL!"

At that moment the door opened.

"Mrs. Carillon! Mrs. Carillon!"

Mrs. Carillon, surprised by the unexpected greeting, dropped three autobiographies and the *American Racing Manual* on her sore feet.

"Mrs. Carillon, we have to pack right away. Next stop: The seals in the New York Zoo."

Next Stop. . .

Mrs. Carillon liked zoos, too; but not enough to return to New York City. On the other hand, she debated, the twins might be right about "C *blub* all = seals." And the most important thing was to find Noel.

"You could hardly have looked at two million men the last time you were there," Tony argued.

"I'll have to think about it for a few days," she said.

"New York City doesn't have just *one* zoo," Tina argued, facts in hand, "it has four zoos and an aquarium."

"I'm still thinking," Mrs. Carillon replied; but the next day she heaved a deep sigh and packed their bags.

****

"Look!" Tony followed Tina's pointing finger out of the front window of the taxi. The skyline of Manhattan soared high above the horizon. Tony gasped and Tina clutched Mrs. Carillon's coat sleeve. There, somewhere among the tall buildings that scraped the sky, they were going to settle down.

The thought of settling down suddenly made the huge city seem less frightening. The twins had never been to New York City before, but somehow, in some way, it seemed like home. They laughed with delight; and Mrs. Carillon managed a weak smile in return.

****

"Home" was a hotel room.

Mrs. Carillon spent afternoons feeding fish to the seals* in the Central Park Zoo, and the twins joined her on Saturday trips, once to the Bronx Zoo and once to the Aquarium. Otherwise, the routine was exactly the same: City Hall, St. Paul's, Chinese restaurants, etc. etc. . . . exactly the same.

One morning at breakfast, only two weeks after their arrival, Mrs. Carillon told the twins of her new plans.

"Tiny," she began. Lately she had fallen into the habit of addressing the twins by that one name. It was easier than saying "Tina and Tony" and better than saying "Tona and Teeny," which she sometimes did.

"Tiny, I think we've made a mistake. You may have been right about 'seals,' but February is a bad time for zoo-going in New York. We'd all be much happier in the South this time of the year. It just so happens that I heard about a zoo in New Orleans. I'll pack the bags while you're in school, and we'll leave right after dinner.

---

* Mrs. Carillon didn't know the difference between seals and sea lions, but no matter. Neither did Noel.

"Next stop," she announced happily, "the Audubon Park Zoo and Odenheimer Aquarium!"

Unhappy St. Valentine's Day*

"Miserable, miserable," Tina muttered, scuffing her shoes along the sidewalk.

"Happy St. Valentine's Day," said Tony, the cheerer-upper.

Tina hadn't forgotten what day it was. She had bought a valentine for Jordan Pinckney, the boy who sat in front of her, and one for Tony.

The class was especially restless, for the handing out of valentines had been saved until the end of the school day. At last the teacher picked an envelope out of the large box on her desk.

"Rosemary Neuberger."

Rosemary Neuberger, the prettiest girl in the class, swished up the aisle and claimed her valentine.

Name after name was called. Tina peeked over Jordan Pinckney's shoulder each time he opened an envelope to see if it was the valentine she had sent. The eighth one was hers; he didn't even turn around.

"Tony Carillon," the teacher called.

Tony pretended he wasn't the least bit interested in this silly ritual. He knew the card was from his sister.

More names and finally, "Tina Carillon."

Tina opened the large envelope slowly and carefully, hoping against hope that it was from Jordan Pinckney. The orange construction paper, neatly lettered "To My

---

* Sad as it may be, this section contains a most important clue
 to . . . .

Valentime" and decorated with red cut-out hearts and a lace paper border, was signed "Tony."

Their names were not called again. Rosemary Neuberger's desk was piled high with twenty-five valentines; others had at least ten. Tina felt that everyone was staring at her one card and one envelope. Tony slipped her his valentine to add to her meager stack.

****

"What long faces!" Mrs. Carillon, still packing, hadn't noticed that the twins were late returning from school. She laid a purple-flowered swimsuit into an open suitcase. "Nobody would guess to look at you two that. . . ."

"We want to go back to the orphanage," Tina blurted out. Her trembling chin forecast tears.

"The orphanage, Teeny?" Mrs. Carillon asked, eyes wide with surprise. "But why?"

The answer was a loud, escaped sob.

Mrs. Carillon turned to Tony, who was staring at his shoes. "Tona?"

"At least we had friends in the orphanage," Tony explained, "but we travel so much now that. . ." He bit his lip, unable to continue.

Mrs. Carillon stepped backward. Slowly, she sat down on the couch, took the crumpled valentines from Tina's fist, and smoothed them out on her knee; all the while trying to put her muddled thoughts in order.

What had she done wrong? She never poked or slapped like Miss Anna Oglethorpe. On the other hand, what had she done right? If only the twins had told her what they wanted. If only Noel were here.

Noel. The twins. Suddenly, Mrs. Carillon realized that

she had two problems, not one; and she knew which was more important. If only it were not too late.

"Tiny?" Mrs. Carillon said warily. "Can I have one more chance?"

Three Italian Dinners and a Horse*

The twins had never eaten in an Italian restaurant before. Neither had Mrs. Carillon. The *antipasto* tasted so good, they couldn't decide whether to eat or talk. They ate and saved their plans for the next course.

Between mouthfuls of *ravioli* Tina announced that she wanted to stay in New York and go to the same school.

Between mouthfuls of *saltimbocca* Mrs. Carillon announced that they would buy a three-bedroom apartment and hire a cook. "And no more traveling, no more face-watching, and no more zoos."

"Watch *glurp* tell *slurp* cow. . ."

"You sound just like Noel. What did you say, Tony?"

Tony swallowed his *fettuccine*. "We can still face-watch on television, and go to cowboy movies and the zoo."

"I never realized how lucky I am," Mrs. Carillon said, beaming on her generous children.

"Can we have a telephone?" Tina asked, hoping that Jordan Pinckney might call her.

"Oh my, you know how my right arm hurts whenever a phone rings. But there I go, thinking only about myself again. Of course we'll get a telephone."

The twins finished their *spumoni* and wiped their smiling mouths.

* Another clue! French is more important than Italian, but an English-language dictionary will do.

"Happy Valentine's Day," Mrs. Carillon said.

They returned to their hotel, but not to sleep. They chatted away about their new plans, ordered up hot chocolate, went to bed, tossed and turned, and got up again. It was two o'clock in the morning, and they were still wide awake.

"Maybe somebody should tell a bedtime story," Tony suggested. He had never heard one.

Neither had Mrs. Carillon, but an expert on horses knows many tales.

****

"Would you like to hear about Christmas Bells?"

The twins shrugged their shoulders. This was no hour to be choosy.

"Well, as you probably know, all famous race horses have famous parents; but not Christmas Bells. That big black stallion was by a nothing, out of a nothing."

The twins were confused by Mrs. Carillon's jargon, but they were too tired to interrupt.

"Christmas Bells was a beautiful horse, but the least bit of exercise left him huffing and puffing. In his first race he not only came in dead last, he walked to the finish line.

"Mr. Hall, his owner, who used to be a famous jockey, was going to sell that lazy horse, when one day he noticed a strange gleam in his eyes. He decided to race Christmas Bells one more time, with he, himself, in the saddle (or 'him up,' as they say)."

Mrs. Carillon was so involved in her story she didn't notice that the twins had fallen asleep.

"*Christmas Bells stepped wearily onto the track. His odds were 50 to 1. His head was bowed low; and it looked as if he might not have the strength to drag himself to the post. His odds went up to 100 to 1.*

"*They're off!*" shouted Mrs. Carillon, startling the twins out of their peaceful slumber. They looked about, and finding everything all right, closed their eyes again.

"*Christmas Bells was the last horse out of the gate. He was twenty lengths back at the first turn, and even more as he neared the far turn. Then, all of a sudden, miracle of miracles, that big black stallion lifted his head, flared his nostrils, and with a fantastic burst of speed, passed horse after horse after horse down the home stretch. And when there was only daylight between him and victory, Christmas Bells broke stride, took two quick little dance steps, turned to look at the people in the stands, then galloped across the finish line.*

"*He won!*" shouted Mrs. Carillon. Tina opened one eye and shut it again.

"*And ever since that amazing day, Christmas Bells has won every. . .*" Mrs. Carillon yawned and saw that her children were fast asleep. She covered them with blankets and went to bed.

Settling Down

They found a large Fifth Avenue apartment with a terrace overlooking Central Park, but Mr. Banks said it was too expensive. "You'd have to own General Motors, not just a soup factory, to afford that one." They moved into a smaller apartment, with no terrace, on Park Avenue.

Mrs. Carillon bought a purple-flowered sofa, purple-flowered chairs, purple-flowered drapes and wallpaper. Her clothes blended in so well with the furniture that the twins had to look twice to be sure she was there.

The twins refused to have purple rooms. "Pink and orange," Tina insisted. Tony couldn't decide what color he wanted for his room. "Anything but purple, and not pink and orange, either." Mrs. Carillon chose red and blue, which looked like purple when she squinted her eyes.

They interviewed dozens of cooks and finally hired Mrs. Baker, a small-boned, thin-lipped woman with mouse-brown hair twisted into a tight bun. She could prepare any dish except soup.

Spring had arrived once again. Mrs. Carillon enjoyed her afternoons feeding the seals* in the Central Park Zoo. She still looked much the same and dressed the same, but she was beginning to smell of fish.

* Sea lions, sea lions, sea lions!

The twins loved New York and their apartment and Mrs. Baker's good cooking. And they had made quite a few friends at school, thanks to Tina's whopping lie.

Tina's Whopping Lie

One afternoon, soon after they had moved into their apartment, Tina and Tony found themselves among a group of bragging classmates.

Jordan Pickney said his father was a famous actor and had just gotten a big part on a television show.

Rosemary Neuberger said that when she was little she got lost at the circus in Madison Square Garden and had to sleep with the elephants.

Mavis Bensonhurst said her mother spent two thousand dollars a year just for underwear.

"Tina and I are twins," was all Tony could think to say. He didn't want anyone to know about the orphanage, or Mrs. Carillon, just yet.

"What's so special about that? I know lots of twins," Rosemary Neuberger said in a voice that made Tony want to hide.

Tina hated Rosemary Neuberger. She hated her as much as she liked Jordan Pinckney, and that was a lot.

"I'll tell you what's so special about that," Tina said. "We're not just ordinary twins. We're Siamese twins. We were born stuck together and weren't cut apart until we were three years old."

"Really?" They were the center of attention now.

"Really!" Tony said proudly.

"Where were you stuck together?" Mavis Bensonhurst wanted to know.

"At our hips." Tony pointed to the spot. "We were connected at our right hips."

"Both of you, at your right hips?" asked Jordan Pinckney, the one doubter in the group.

Tina immediately recognized Tony's error. "That's right. My right hip was joined to Tony's right hip. When I faced front, he faced back; and when I faced back, he faced front."

"Then how could you walk?"

"In circles!" Tina said triumphantly.

"Wow!"

Word spread quickly. Everyone wanted a friend who was a Siamese twin.

Same Old Argument

Mr. Banks was waiting in the living room when Mrs. Carillon returned from the zoo. He shook his head and tsk-tsked over a stack of bills.

"Six handmade silk dresses, ten handmade pairs of shoes, and look at this: a case of Burgundy Bash lipsticks made to order. Mrs. Carillon, you are too extravagant, much too extravagant."

Mrs. Carillon explained that she had gained weight and her old dresses no longer fit; her shoes were walked clean through; and lipsticks don't last forever. Everything had to be custom-made because the things she wore weren't manufactured anymore.

"You don't seem to understand, Mr. Banks," she explained. "If I don't dress the same as always, Noel might not recognize me."

Mr. Banks slammed the bills down on the table.

"When are you going to come to your senses and give up this ridiculous search?"

Mrs. Carillon, used to Mr. Banks' frequent outbursts, ignored the question. Instead, she promised not to eat so much of Mrs. Baker's good cooking.

"Mrs. Carillon, I've told you time and again. . ." Tina whispered in Tony's ear, knowing exactly what the next words would be.

"Mrs. Carillon, I've told you time and again," Mr. Banks shouted, "Noel must be dead, or he'd have asked for money by now. Anyhow, he's been missing so long that he's legally dead."

"The law has nothing to do with it," Tina whispered.

"The law has nothing to do with it," Mrs. Carillon said. "My husband is my husband, until I find out otherwise."

Mrs. Carillon's reply, about Noel having amnesia and being poor and sick and needing her, was mouthed word for word by Tina. Tony tried not to giggle, but a loud snort escaped.

"Young man, I don't see what's so funny," Mr. Banks hissed.

Tony lost all control. He laughed so hard he doubled over and rolled on the floor.

Tina had to act quickly. "Mr. Banks," she said sweetly, "won't you stay for dinner?"

Mr. Banks looked at Tina standing before him in wide-eyed innocence.

"At least there's one sane person in this family," he said.

****

Tina and Tony really didn't dislike Mr. Banks. They just found this tight-collared, tight-vested, gray-haired, gray-suited man boring. He talked only about money, and he never laughed. He ate heartily, though, and the twins were surprised when he actually smiled and said, "Best meal I've had since my wife died ten years ago."

He never watched television, of course, and left right after dinner.

Cardinals vs. Mets

For an hour, every evening after dinner, the twins watched television with Mrs. Carillon. They scanned the faces and neckties of men in the local news, national news, and international news; men in picket lines, parades, and demonstrations. They even watched commercials.

"Who knows but some soap company might want a handsome man like Noel to tell housewives what soap to use in their washing machines," Mrs. Carillon would say. "Or maybe some razor-blade company might pay Noel to shave off his red moustache on television."

Sports news was their favorite, though. Whenever the announcer said, "The feature race was won by Christmas Bells," Tina and Mrs. Carillon let out a lusty cheer. Tony was more interested in baseball.

"The St. Louis Cardinals are playing the Mets at Shea Stadium tonight," Tony said. "And the game is going to be on television."

"Wouldn't you rather go to the movies?" Mrs. Carillon asked, her eyes still glued to the set. "We usually go to a cowboy movie on Fridays."

Tony couldn't make up his mind.

"Tina, what would you like to do?" Mrs. Carillon asked. "Tina?"

Tina was deep in thought. "One minute, I've almost got it, except for the 'I *glub*.' "

Mrs. Carillon turned away from the television set to stare at Tina. "What have you got?"

" 'C *blub* all' could mean 'St. Louis Cardinals' and 'new. . . .' could mean 'New York Mets.' "

"Tina, that's wonderful!" Mrs. Carillon decided to stay home and watch the ball game.

Tony didn't think Tina's idea was at all wonderful. Noel had said that in December, and major league baseball isn't played in winter. Besides, the Mets weren't around twenty-one years ago. Football was a possibility, but Tony didn't mention any of this. He had decided he wanted to watch the game.

****

Mrs. Carillon disappeared into the purple-flowered couch. The twins sat on either side of her, waiting for the first pitch.

It was a strike.

"Oh, no!" Mrs. Carillon sighed.

"That's good," Tony explained. "The Cardinals are at bat. We're for the other side."

"It's just that I realized Noel is too old to be a ball player."

The batter hit a high foul into the stands. The camera followed the ball as it bounced off the fingertips of one fan into the hands of another. The crowd around him waved at the unseen television audience.

"Look at all those faces," Mrs. Carillon exclaimed with renewed interest.

The batter struck out, as did the next, and the third man popped up to short.

"We don't have to watch that," Mrs. Carillon said when the commercial was shown. "Noel is too genteel to drink beer."

The Mets came up to bat; three easy outs. The first inning was over.

"My word, look at that! Look at all those banners: 'Let's Go Mets,' 'Massapequa Loves the Mets.' " Mrs. Carillon read aloud from the boldly lettered bedsheets held aloft by the fans. "Tiny, look carefully for 'Noel Carillon Loves the Mets.' "

****

"No luck tonight," she said after the Mets won the game in the tenth inning. "I must have looked at 20,000 faces and read 150 signs. We'll have to watch again tomorrow."

"I have a better idea," Tony said. "Let's go to Shea Stadium with our own bedsheet: 'Noel: Call Mrs. Carillon, SH 1-1212.' "

"We can't do that," Tina said. "Every crank* in town will call our number."

"Tina's right," Mrs. Carillon was quick to agree.

Tony had another suggestion. "How about: 'Mrs. Carillon Is Here!'? When Noel sees that he'll come to the next ball game and find us."

"What if Noel has a black-and-white TV set?" Tina asked.

"What difference does that make?"

"If he has a black-and-white set he won't be able to read a sign lettered on a purple-flowered bedsheet, or

* SH 1-1212 is not Mrs. Carillon's real phone number. It was changed here just in case some crank knows how to read.

even an orange one, or a navy blue one. We don't have a white bedsheet in the house."

"No problem," Mrs. Carillon said. "First thing tomorrow, we'll go to Bloomingdale's and buy some white sheets."

Bedlam in Bloomingdale's*

Mrs. Carillon and the twins were riding the Up escalator to the second floor, when Tony shouted, "Look! A red moustache and sunglasses!"

"And a black tie!" Tina pointed to a man in a tan raincoat moving past them on the Down escalator.

Mrs. Carillon spun about in time to see the back of the head of a tall, thin man with brown hair. "Leon!"

No one moved.

"Fire on the second floor," Tina shouted, "everybody turn around and go down! Fire!"

Now they moved. Panic spread quickly as Tina's words were echoed by the near-hysterical passengers on the Up escalator. "Fire, fire, turn around!" People pushed and shoved, trying to step down as the stairs moved up.

"We're not getting anywhere," cried Mrs. Carillon as she saw Noel heading for the front door.

"Hurry! One, two, one, two!" Tony shouted, counting a pace faster than the rate of the moving stairs.

The crowd began surging downward. Unfortunately, a shopper couldn't manage her footing at the landing. She fell on the rising step and almost rode back up the escalator on her belly; but the next person fell on her, and the next and the next.

"Jump, Mrs. Carillon, jump!" Tony shouted, as he and

* Mrs. Carillon runs into someone very important to her. Guess who.

Tina crawled over the scrambled pile of struggling shoppers.

Mrs. Carillon took a flying leap across the heap of people, landed on her knees, picked herself up, and started running for the door. "Leon, Noel!"

Suddenly, she was jerked to an abrupt halt. "Let me go, let me go!" she screamed, pummeling a pudgy man in rimless glasses whose cuff button was caught in her fishnet bag.

"I'm s-s-so s-s-sorry," he stammered, nervously trying to undo his button.

Mrs. Carillon couldn't wait. She turned toward the door and started running again, lurching the ensnared man off his feet and dragging him backward, his arm still linked to the fishnet bag, his legs high in the air, the seat of his pants skidding along the floor. It never occurred to Mrs. Carillon, as she pushed and shoved her way through the crowd, to let go of her bag.

"Oof!" The pudgy man's head hit the bottom of a counter, bringing him to a painful stop. The fishnet bag tore, propelling Mrs. Carillon into a skinny, little man with a ratlike face. He was no match for Mrs. Carillon, who fell on top of him to the crash of broken glass and the stifling odor of heavy perfume.

"Fire, fire!"

The heap of people at the bottom of the escalator had untangled themselves and were running wildly for the door, shouting their warning to the other customers.

The first woman in the frantic mob tripped and fell on top of Mrs. Carillon and the rat-faced man, the next one fell on her, and once again, the next and the next. The crush of bodies and the strong perfume were too much for Mrs. Carillon. She fainted.

The Chase

Tina and Tony ran down Lexington Avenue, dodging
shoppers and strollers, every now and then catching a
glimpse of the man in the tan raincoat. He crossed Fifty-
eighth Street and turned left—no, right. There were two
tan raincoats.

Tony couldn't make up his mind which way to go.

"You go right; I'll go left," Tina said. "Meet you back
at Bloomingdale's."

Tina lost her man in the tan raincoat one block later,
but Tony kept up his chase, down Fifty-seventh Street, in
and out of Hammacher Schlemmer's, to Third Avenue,
left. He almost caught up with him at Fifty-ninth Street,
but the traffic light changed. Tony climbed up the light
standard for a better view; the tan raincoat disappeared
into the back entrance of Bloomingdale's. The Walk sign
flashed on. Tony dashed across the street and into the
store.

There he was, in Men's Pajamas.

"Mr. Carillon!" Tony grabbed the raincoat just in case
Noel had any ideas of escaping again.

The tall man looked down at Tony, his puzzled smile
half-hidden by a bushy black moustache.

"Sorry," Tony said.

The Bearded Beggar

Tony found Tina at the front entrance of the store. She
was wearing her "miserable" expression.

"We're miserable orphans again," she said. "Mrs. Carillon's been arrested for inciting a riot. She's in jail."

"Poor Mrs. Carillon. Maybe we can bail her out."

"It's no use. Today is Saturday. We can't reach Mr. Banks until Monday, and all I've got is eight cents."

Tony had five cents. "Where's the jail?"

"Greenwich Avenue and Eighth Street. We don't even have enough money for the subway."

"Maybe we can borrow the money. Start crying so somebody will feel sorry for us."

Tina screwed up her face; nothing happened. "I'm too miserable to cry."

"Then stop making faces. No one will give us even two cents if you look like that. Hey, look at that guy!" Tony pointed to a barefoot young man with long hair and a straggly beard who was holding out his hand to a matronly shopper.

"I need $2.50 to get to New Jersey," he said.

"Get a haircut," the woman replied.

"I need $2.50 to get to New Jersey," he said to a passing secretary. She opened her purse and gave him 50 cents.

"Let's try it," Tony said. They approached an old woman. "We need some money to get to jail."

The old woman walked on. They tried a younger woman, then a man. No one took any notice of them.

"Get a job like everybody else," someone said to the bearded young man, but the next woman gave him a dollar.

"Did you see that?" Tony said. "A dollar!"

"I've been counting how much he's made," Tina said, "and it's more than $2.50. Let's ask *him* for money."

Tony shyly approached the barefoot beggar, taking care not to step on his toes. "Please, sir, could we have a dollar?"

"Hey, that's beautiful," laughed the hairy young man, whose name was Harry. "But you're not playing the game right. First off, you're too well dressed. Now if. . . ."

This was too much for Tina. She had no trouble crying this time.

"I'm sorry, kids. Are you in some kind of trouble?" Harry put his hands on Tony's shoulders. "I'll give you a dollar. Just tell me what you need it for."

"To see our mother in jail."

"In jail? Where's your dad?"

"We're orphans," Tina blurted out.

"You kids need more than a dollar, you need real help. We'll stop off and see some friends of mine on the way to the prison."

Harry took the twins by the hands and led them down the subway stairs. On the ride to Astor Place, Tony told him the story of Mrs. Carillon's arrest.

Friends in Need

Tina and Tony followed Harry up five flights of dingy stairs to a large loft. "Hold everything," he shouted over the din of a sculptor hammering on a rusty piece of iron. The four artists in the room looked up from their work and saw the unhappy twins.

"This is Tina and this is Tony. Their mother was arrested in Bloomingdale's for inciting a riot," Harry explained.

"What was she protesting?" asked Joel, a tall man with a large puff of black hair.

"She just tripped and fell and that made other people fall," Tina said, afraid to admit that she was the one who had incited the riot by yelling "Fire," not Mrs. Carillon.

"Injustice!" proclaimed a girl with long brown hair and red beads. The others agreed.

"She's locked up in the Women's House of Detention," Harry added.

"That pest-hole!"

Tears started in Tina's eyes as she pictured poor Mrs. Carillon in a pest-hole. She decided to give herself up to the police as soon as they reached the jail.

"Don't worry, kids, we'll get your mother out of there," Joel promised. "Everybody, find some poster board and start making signs. We're going to march on the prison."

"What's your mother's name?" asked the girl with the beads, brush in hand.

"Mrs. Carillon. C-a-r-i-l-l-o-n."

The artists worked quickly. Tina watched with awe as the bold brushstrokes formed letters, then words. Tony walked from easel to easel, reading the signs aloud:

FREE MRS. CARILLON
FREE THE ORPHANS' MOTHER
WOMEN'S HOUSE OF DETENTION IS A PEST-HOLE
GRAPE MRS. CARILLON

"Grape Mrs. Carillon?" Joel exclaimed. "What is *that* supposed to mean?"

The girl with the red beads stared at the poster on which she had just lettered "Mrs. Carillon." "I guess this sign was left over from the grape workers' boycott," she said sheepishly. "I didn't notice. . ."

"Well, no time to change it now. Everybody ready?"

The protest march was about to begin.

Grape Mrs. Carillon!

Tina rode on Harry's shoulders, Tony on Joel's, as the march proceeded single-file up Eighth Street. Joel started to chant, "Free Mrs. Carillon," and the others joined in. Two long-haired girls joined the line; then a bearded man in sandals; then five young men with shaven heads and long saffron robes who beat a rhythmic step with cymbals, castanets, and bongo drum.

Tony chanted along with his new friends, but Tina was too nervous to do anything but bite her nails. If the protest march didn't work, she, too, would have to spend the weekend in a pest-hole.

"Harry?" she asked in a choked-up voice, "What's a pest-hole?"

"Just what it sounds like. That jail is filthy with pests: cockroaches, bedbugs, rats."

Tina sorted out the filthy pests in her mind. She knew all about cockroaches, everybody in New York did. You stepped on them or hit them with a shoe, and sometimes you squashed one, and sometimes it would escape. She could handle those bugs, as long as there weren't too many. Just in case, she would buy a can of roach powder before she made her confession. But what about the bedbugs?

"Have you ever seen a bedbug, Harry?"

"Can't say that I have. Bedbugs are shy creatures; they only come out at night when it is dark and everyone is asleep."

"Shy creatures" didn't sound too horrible. But rats! It was the miserable rats that scared her to death. Tina shivered at the thought.

"Harry, did the grape workers win?"

"Yep, they sure did."

Tina breathed a sigh of relief. If Harry and his friends could help the grape workers, they could certainly help Mrs. Carillon.

"Harry, how long did it take for the grape workers to win?"

"Five years."

Tina started to shiver again.

****

"Free Mrs. Carillon! Free Mrs. Carillon!"

The chanting grew louder as the protesters neared the prison, but not loud enough to drown out a whining voice from the sidelines.

"Would you look at that! Did you ever see anything so disgusting? I'd like to stick them all in a bathtub and cut their hair."

Tony turned toward the shrill voice and saw two over-dressed, overstuffed women shaking their heads at the straggly marchers.

"And just take a look at that filthy language," the voice continued. " 'Grape Mrs. Carillon' it says. There should be a law."

"What does 'grape' mean?" her companion asked.

"You can well imagine what such filth means. It's obscene, that's what it is, foul and obscene."

Tony wondered how anybody could be so mean. Couldn't that silly woman see that his friends were trying to free his mother from jail, or didn't she care?

"Indecent!" she shrieked. "You all belong in jail!"

That was more than Tony could stand.

"Grape Mrs. Carillon!" he shouted. He turned and

stared into the hateful woman's shocked face. "AND GRAPE YOU!"

Tina was still worrying about the rats, but Tony felt much better.

A Familiar Arm

"Free Mrs. Carillon!" the thirty members of the Ad Hoc Committee to Free the Orphans' Mother shouted from the triangular traffic island facing the prison.

Tina and Tony, high on their friends' shoulders, peered over the picket signs at the massive brick fortress, The Women's House of Detention, the "pest-hole," that towered over the quaint neighborhood of small shops.

"Free Mrs. Carillon! Free Mrs. Carillon!"

The rhythmic chant grew louder and louder. It soared over the noise of the traffic, up to the top of the prison. Outstretched arms of the women inmates waved at the protesters through the barred fence of the recreation yard on the roof of the jail.

"There she is! There's Mrs. Carillon!" Tina cried, pointing to a plump arm waving a purple-flowered hand-kerchief.

"Free Mrs. Carillon! Free the orphans' mother!"

****

"She's gone!" gasped Tina. She searched for the familiar handkerchief among the waving arms, but it was no longer there.

"Maybe they put her in solitary," suggested an alarmed Tony.

"Maybe she's been eaten by a rat," Tina shrieked. "Let me down, let me down! I want to confess!"

"Look!" All eyes followed Tony's pointing finger. A plump woman in a purple-flowered dress emerged from the green copper gate of the prison. "It's Mrs. Carillon!"

Fortunately, a policeman had halted all traffic, for Mrs. Carillon raced across the street to the traffic island without looking left or right. The twins were set down just as she arrived to clutch them in her arms.

In the midst of the laughing and shouting Tony suddenly remembered his friends. "Mrs. Carillon, this is Joel and this is Harry. They rescued you from the 'pesthole.' "

Mrs. Carillon grasped their hands between hers. "How can I ever thank you?"

"It was the least we could do," answered Harry. "You are a martyr, Mrs. Carillon."

"A martyr?" she said in surprise. "I thought you had to be dead to be a martyr."

"You are a *living* martyr, Mrs. Carillon," Joel replied.

****

Traffic was moving again. Harry hailed a passing taxi and the weary threesome got in.

"One minute," Mrs. Carillon said to the driver. She rolled down the window and called to Harry. "Maybe you can help my cellmate, Mineola Potts. She's such a nice lady."

"What's she in for?"

"Jaywalking."

No one noticed the pudgy man* with rimless glasses and bandaged head who hurried out of the prison after Mrs. Carillon. No one heard him shout after the taxi, for the chant, "Free Mineola Potts," was in full swell.

* Guess again.

"Was she really arrested for jaywalking?" Tony asked.

"Indeed she was, poor woman," Mrs. Carillon replied. "She was very hungry and had nothing to eat, so she borrowed two cans of lobster meat and a tin of caviar from the supermarket. She was jaywalking when the police stopped her."

Tina sighed over the unhappy plight of poor, miserable Mineola Potts.

You!

Mrs. Carillon wanted to go home and jump into a hot tub, but was outvoted by the tired but hungrier twins, who insisted on describing their day's adventure in full detail over hamburgers and ice cream sodas.

When they finally arrived at their apartment, Mrs. Baker greeted them with the news that they had a visitor.

"He's been sitting there in the living room for an hour. He doesn't say anything, just sits."

Tina and Tony exchanged anxious glances. The only visitor they ever had was Mr. Banks, and he didn't count. Tina asked the question they were all thinking.

"Does he have a red moustache and a black tie?"

"Nope," said Mrs. Baker.

The short, pudgy man with rimless glasses and band-aged head rose timidly from his chair when they entered the room. "Mrs. C-C-Carillon, I. . ."

"You!" shouted Mrs. Carillon, pointing a menacing finger at the man whose cuff button had caught in her fishnet bag. "You!"

Mrs. Carillon's finger made the little man so nervous he could scarcely speak. His words tripped over one another, then refused to come out at all.

Tina felt sorry for him, whoever he might be. "Won't you sit down?" she said graciously.

Tony stayed close to Mrs. Carillon's side to protect her from this unwelcome stranger, who nodded and smiled shyly at Tina but remained standing.

Mrs. Carillon studied him carefully. He looked harmless enough. Besides, there was something about him that reminded her of someone, but she couldn't remember who.

"Well, what's done is done," she said with a sigh and wearily dropped into an armchair. Only then did her nervous guest sit down.

He began to stammer and stutter again, but finally, painfully, he delivered his message. He had come to apologize for the inconvenience he had caused Mrs. Carillon in Bloomingdale's. He hoped she didn't think he had done it deliberately.

Mrs. Carillon was forgiving.

He had tried to undo his cuff button from her fishnet bag; in the confusion he had only made it worse.

Mrs. Carillon was understanding.

He would have come to her aid sooner, but he was rushed to the hospital to have sixteen stitches put in his forehead.

Mrs. Carillon was sympathetic.

He was pleased that he had not been too late to put up bail in time to. . ."

"Bail?" Mrs. Carillon exclaimed.

"I thought the protest marchers freed Mrs. Carillon," Tina said.

"Oh, n-n-no. I was happy to see that you have so m-m-many friends; but there are legal f-f-formalities, you know."

"Then I'm not a living martyr after all."

"Living m-m-martyr?" He had never heard that expression before. "You will have to face t-t-trial, so. . . ."

"Trial?" Tina gasped, once again riddled with guilt.

"Trial?" echoed Mrs. Carillon.

It was up to Tony to play host. "My name is Tony and this is my sister Tina. What's yours?"

The nervous man gave a nervous smile, which no one returned. "D-d-don't you recognize me, Mrs. C-C-Carillon?"

Once again she studied the familiar face.

"Augie Kunkel!"

"Mrs. C-C-Carillon!"

They leaped from their seats and met in the middle of the room. Mrs. Carillon grabbed Augie Kunkel's hands.

"Augie Kunkel," she repeated.

"Mrs. C-C-Carillon."

The joyous reunion didn't last long; they couldn't think of anything else to say.

Mrs. Carillon dropped her old friend's hands and sank back into her chair. Augie Kunkel was well aware of her weariness. He made an awkward exit, taking short little bows while backing out toward the door. Mrs. Carillon watched her childhood playmate about to leave and was overcome with gratitude.

"Good night, Augie," she said. "And thank you for everything. Won't you join us for dinner tomorrow evening?"

Augie Kunkel's face lit up with a broad smile, "a nice smile," thought Mrs. Carillon. "Six o'clock, then," she said as Tina closed the door after him.

"What a kind man," Mrs. Carillon said. "What a shy creature."

"Shy creature," Tina repeated, half-asleep. "Like a bedbug."

"Tina!"

A Namer of Things

Mr. Kunkel arrived on the dot of six, a few minutes after Mrs. Carillon returned from feeding the sea lions.

"So good of you to come, Augie," she said.

Augie tried to think of something clever to say, but all that came out was a stammered, "F-f-fish?"

"Roast duck," Tony answered.

"Strange, I c-c-could have sworn I smelled f-f-fish." Too flustered to look at anyone, Mr. Kunkel began to examine the objects in the living room.

"A violet-glazed figure of the K'ang Hsi," he said clearly and with authority.

"A pair of molded *flaschenhalter*," he continued.

Tina was surprised that he wasn't stuttering anymore; Tony was amazed that one person could know so much; and Mrs. Carillon was delighted to learn that her objects had names.

"*Blanc de Chine* triple lichee box, a Regency carved giltwood *fauteuil*."

"How do you know all that?" Tony asked.

"Oh, I read b-b-books and know how to look things up. I like to know the n-n-names of everything I see: t-t-trees, flowers, furniture, everything."

"Does naming help you make up your mind about things?" Tony needed all the help he could get in this department.

"N-n-no, not really. I just n-n-name things; I n-n-never go so far as to form an opinion." Mr. Kunkel stared down at the Oriental rug. *"Hamadan Serebend."* He looked up at Tony and smiled shyly.

Tony had decided one thing: he liked Augie Kunkel. "I don't see why everyone is supposed to have an opinion about everything all the time, anyway."

"Dinner is served," Tina announced upon a signal from Mrs. Baker.

****

"Caneton à l'orange, petits pois, purée de pommes de terre." Augie Kunkel named the duck, peas, and mashed potatoes, then turned to Mrs. Carillon. "T-t-tell me about Leon."

"Noel," Tina said.

Mrs. Carillon told about her long search for her missing husband as quickly as possible, for the story always made her sad.

"P-p-poor Little Dumpling."

The sound of her old nickname made Mrs. Carillon even sadder; but the twins, who had never heard it before, burst into convulsive giggles. Their laughter was finally cut short by the disapproving stare of Mrs. Baker arriving with a platter of second portions.

"More duck, Tony?"

"I don't care," he answered as usual.

"Yes or no," Mrs. Baker insisted.

"That is q-q-quite a difficult decision if T-T-Tony doesn't know what the d-d-dessert is," said Mr. Kunkel, coming to the rescue.

"Peaches with ice cream," replied Mrs. Baker.

"No, thank you," said Tony, beaming at his new friend, "no more duck."

"Tell me about yourself, Augie," Mrs. Carillon said. "Is naming things a good job?"

"I don't make my living n-n-naming things," Augie answered gently. "It's what you m-m-might call a hobby."

"What do you do?" Tony asked. Whatever it was, that was what Tony wanted to do, unless he had to be fat to do it.

"I invent crossword puzzles."

"Crossword puzzles!" Tina exclaimed. "You're just the person we need to solve the *glub-blubs*."

I Never Wear Underwear

Mrs. Carillon sighed on hearing *glub-blubs*; she was sad again. And the sadder Mrs. Carillon became, the guiltier Tina felt.

"What would you like for Mother's Day," Tina asked to cheer her up.

"Mother's Day?" Mrs. Carillon said, brightening. "Why, I've never ever received a Mother's Day present before."

"How about lace underwear?" Tina suggested. "Mavis Bensonhurst's mother always wears lace underwear in case she's hit by a truck and her dress flies up in the air."

"That's stupid," Tony said. "If Mavis Bensonhurst's mother were hit by a truck, she wouldn't know the difference; she'd be dead."

"Nevertheless," Mrs. Carillon said, "some women do feel that way. I often think of that myself; that's why I never wear any underwear at all."

Tina's mouth dropped open. Tony's face turned a bright red. Augie Kunkel cleared his throat and lowered his eyes.

"You really don't mean that, Mrs. Carillon," Tina said. "You're only joking, aren't you, Mrs. Carillon?"

"Why should I joke about such a thing?" Mrs. Carillon replied, unaware of the confusion she had caused. "If I said I never wear underwear, that means I never wear underwear."

Tina couldn't believe her ears. Tony wanted to die of embarrassment. The twins expected Mr. Kunkel to leave the table in shocked outrage; but he just sat there, intently polishing his glasses with his greasy napkin.

"Why, I haven't worn underwear in over twenty years," Mrs. Carillon explained. "I wear a bathing suit, instead. That way, if I'm ever hit by a truck and my skirt flies over my head, Noel would recognize the purple flowers. And, if he wasn't at the scene of the accident, he would read in the paper:

UNIDENTIFIED WOMAN IN PURPLE-FLOWERED SWIMSUIT
HIT BY TRUCK.

"Do you always wear the same bathing suit?" Tony asked, not quite sure that it still wasn't indecent.

"Oh no, dear, not the same one. I change every day. I own twenty-four of them, all exactly the same."

The twins broke into giggles again. So did Augie Kunkel.

"What's so funny?" Mrs. Carillon asked, which made them laugh even harder. She joined in with a few bewildered chuckles and waited until they were all laughed out.

"Let's have dessert in the living room," she said, rising from her chair.

Augie Kunkel leaped up to offer her his arm, but he couldn't see a thing through his grease-smeared glasses. He tripped over his chair and fell, hitting his head on the corner of the table.

Mrs. Carillon screamed. Tony knelt down and held his hand. Tina called Dr. Stein who called an ambulance. Augie Kunkel was rushed to the hospital to have fourteen more stitches put in his head.

Good News and a Cheese

"What a miserable day," Tina said on the way home from school.

Tony agreed. Rosemary Neuberger had laughed out loud at him in class, because he couldn't decide whether the Spanish Inquisition was good or bad.

"I don't think I feel so good," Tina said, opening the front door. "I think I'll go right to bed." Jordan Pinckney had told her that Siamese twins had to be either both girls or both boys. As if she didn't have enough to worry about, what with the confession she had to make before the upcoming trial.

"Mr. Kunkel!" Tony was delighted to see him sitting in the living room having tea with Mrs. Carillon.

"Mr. Kunkel, what *are* you wearing?" Tina asked.

"Oh, this?" He pointed to the football helmet on his head. "My d-d-doctor said I have to wear this for a few months. One more accident, he said, and my b-b-brains would end up scrambled eggs."

"And it's all my fault," Mrs. Carillon said.

"N-n-not at all, my p-p-problems are minuscule compared to yours."

Tony repeated "minuscule" under his breath. It was a good word; he liked it.

The telephone rang.

"Oh, ow, ouch!" cried Mrs. Carillon, grabbing her right arm.

"G-g-good grief, what happened?" Augie Kunkel ran to Mrs. Carillon's aid as Tony ran to answer the telephone before the second ring.

"Hello. . . ? Yes. . . One minute, please." Tony placed his hand over the receiver. "Mrs. Carillon, it's for you. It's the manager of Bloomingdale's."

Tina blanched.

Mrs. Carillon bounded up from her seat, stood absolutely still, and plopped back onto the couch again.

"I just can't . . . it's probably something awful." Her voice was trembling. "Augie, would you?"

"Of c-c-course." He gave her a reassuring smile and took the phone from Tony.

"Hello, hello. . . ? What did you say. . . ? I can't hear you."

Tony pointed to the football helmet.

"One moment, p-p-please." Augie Kunkel removed the helmet with a sheepish grin. "N-n-now, then, would you repeat that. . . ? Yes. . . Yes. . . Yes. . . Yes. . . Yes. . . Yes. . . Yes, that is very k-k-kind of you. . . . Yes. . . Yes, I'll give her the m-m-message. Thank you, good-by."

"What is it? What did he say?" Tina asked impatiently as Mr. Kunkel carefully replaced the helmet on his head.

"Everything is q-q-quite all right," he said finally. "In fact, everything is just fine. It seems, Mrs. C-C-Carillon, that when you fell on the little rat-faced man you did B-B-Bloomingdale's a great favor. That man was Ambrose Ambergris, the notorious perfume thief the police have been trying to catch for years. B-B-Bloomingdale's is extremely g-g-grateful. Not only have they d-d-dropped all charges against you, they are sending you a year's free supply of C-C-Camembert cheese."

"Does that mean there's not going to be a trial?" Tina asked.

"That's right; n-n-no trial."

"Whew!"

Mrs. Carillon also breathed a sigh of relief. "I never did enjoy being a living martyr."

"You may not be a living m-m-martyr, Mrs. Carillon, but you are a heroine. And I would like to take everyone to an Armenian restaurant for dinner. We have some celebrating to d-d-do."

Mrs. Carillon and the twins eagerly accepted the invitation. They certainly did have something to celebrate, for a change.

An Unwelcome Guest

"I'm going to celebrate the most," Tina said; and then the doorbell rang.

Tony was almost trampled underfoot by a raging Mr. Banks waving a newspaper in the air and shouting, "Where is she?"

"Are you looking for me?" Mrs. Carillon asked.

"This is too much, too much," he shouted after having distinguished the purple-flowered Mrs. Carillon from the purple-flowered furniture. "Your ridiculous capers are plastered all over the newspapers.

"Just look at this!" Mr. Banks slapped the back of his hand against the front page and read aloud:

SOUP HEIRESS INCITES RIOT IN BLOOMINGDALE'S
HIPPIES DEMONSTRATE TO FREE MRS. CARILLON.

"How wonderful," said Mrs. Carillon, standing on tiptoe to read over Mr. Banks' shoulder.

"Maybe Leon will see the headlines and. . ."

"Leon, Leon, that's all you ever think about!"

"Noel," corrected Tina.

"You stay out of this, young lady." Mr. Banks pointed an accusing finger at Tina. Mrs. Carillon reached for the newspaper to read about her adventure, but Mr. Banks whipped it away and turned his menacing finger toward her.

"Enough of this insane search. You're not only making a silly fool out of yourself; you're ruining the business to boot. You'll be lucky if I can get the charge reduced to disturbing the peace."

"One m-m-minute," stammered Augie Kunkel. "I m-m-must ask you to lower your voice, or, or, or leave this house at once."

"And who do you think you are, tight end for the Green Bay Packers?"

"Why, Mr. Banks," said Mrs. Carillon, not the least ruffled by his violent show of temper, "don't you remember Augie Kunkel?"

"Mr. Kunkel took care of everything," Tony explained. "He arranged bail and made Bloomingdale's drop the case. And he's not a football player. Mr. Kunkel hurt his head helping Mrs. Carillon."

It was somewhat of an exaggeration, but it calmed down Mr. Banks.

"Why doesn't everybody sit down and relax for a few minutes," Mrs. Carillon suggested, having gotten possession of the newspaper at last.

****

"August Kunkel, now I remember," Mr. Banks said. "Your father was foreman at the factory until the tragedy. A good man, your father. He worked hard to make Mrs. Carillon's Pomato Soup the success it is today."

"Are you Mr. Kunkel's trustee, too?" Tony asked.

"No, of course not. Mr. Kunkel's father didn't have any money. He didn't own the business, you know; he just worked for it."

"There was a little insurance m-m-money," Augie Kunkel explained. "I went to live with my m-m-maiden aunt."

"If Mr. Kunkel's father worked so hard for the business, he should have owned part of it, too," Tony said.

"Young man, you know nothing about business," Mr. Banks said uneasily. "What do they teach you at that school, anyway? Socialism?"

"No, the Spanish Inquisition," answered Tony, who had decided it was a bad thing after witnessing Mr. Banks' earlier performance.

The subject of school reminded Tina of another problem. "Mr. Kunkel, what is the name of a boy and girl who are Siamese twins?"

"That's impossible," said Mr. Banks. "Siamese twins are either two boys or two girls."

"I asked Mr. Kunkel," Tina said, trying not to show her annoyance. "What if there *were* such a thing, Mr. Kunkel, what would you call it?"

"You can't have a name for something that doesn't exist," Mr. Banks insisted. "Just what *are* they teaching you at that school?"

"Mr. Kunkel?" Tina tried again in desperation.

"I g-g-guess I would call it a medical phenomenon," Augie Kunkel said, to Tina's satisfaction.

Mrs. Carillon looked up from the newspapers. "Good heavens, what do I smell?"

"I thought it was fish," Mr. Banks said, "but now I think it's pot roast."

"Oh, Mrs. Baker," Mrs. Carillon called to the kitchen. "I'm sorry. I forgot to tell you we're not eating home."

"And waste all that good food!" Mr. Banks was off on one of his "extravagance" lectures again. The celebrants beat a hasty retreat to the door, leaving him with an audience of one, the annoyed Mrs. Baker.

7* Noel _____ C _____ all / I _____ new. . . .

An Armenian Dinner*

"Kouzou kezartma, yaprak dolma. . ." Augie Kunkel and Tony chanted names of Armenian dishes in time to the bouzouki music, and Mrs. Carillon contributed a finger-snapping accompaniment.

Tina toyed with her stuffed grape leaves.

"Tina, dear, aren't you hungry?" Mrs. Carillon asked.

"She's probably feeling sorry for the perfume thief," Tony suggested, but Augie Kunkel knew the real reason for her discomfort.

"Why don't we start working on the *glub-blubs*," he said, handing her a pen and paper.

Tina soon forgot that everyone in the restaurant was staring at their noisy party, and especially at Mr. Kunkel, who wore his football helmet throughout dinner. She carefully wrote out Noel's last message:

Noel *glub* C *blub* all. . .I *glub* new. . . .

All of a sudden their table was the quietest one in the restaurant. Mrs. Carillon and the twins studied Mr. Kunkel study the *glub-blubs*. At one point he said, "Hmmm," and the three of them held their breath; but he was silent again for another ten minutes.

---

* This section is for puzzle-people. Horse-lovers may skip to page 94 and continue reading.

"We have so little to go on," he said finally. "We do know that Noel had a nice word sense, for 'Noel' is 'Leon' spelled backward."

Mrs. Carillon was invisibly lettering "Leon" and "Noel" on the tablecloth with her fingernail to see if they really were the same backward as forward. "Pardon?"

"I said, just four questions," Augie Kunkel repeated. "First, are you sure you called out 'Leon' instead of 'Noel'?"

"I think so," said Mrs. Carillon.

"I know so," said Tina.

"All right, then," Augie Kunkel said, "we will presume that: *the first word is 'Noel.'* *

'Next question: Are you sure there was no sound between 'all' and 'I'?"

"Quite sure. Leon, I mean Noel, went under water there without so much as a *blub*."

"Good, then we will presume that: *the message has two parts.*

"Third question: Was 'new' the end of the message?"

"I don't know. It was the last sound I heard before I was hit on the head."

Augie Kunkel nodded sympathetically. "I know how that can feel. It does make it more difficult, though, not knowing how many words, if any, follow 'new'; but at least we can write the message in a simpler form."

Noel _____ C _____ all / I _____ new. . . .

"That does look easier," Tina remarked.

"One more question," Augie Kunkel said. "Would you say that Noel used precise language?"

---

* If you want to complicate matters you can work with the two sounds: "No" (or "know") and "el" (or "L.").

"Precise? I think so," Mrs. Carillon replied. "Would you like to hear the other messages?"

"If they are not too personal."

"The first message said, 'Hi.' "

"That certainly is precise."

Mrs. Carillon recited all of Noel's messages, including the hotel note.

Augie Kunkel beamed. "Wonderful. You have given me a very important clue."

Syllable Counting

"I gave you a clue?"

"Indeed you did, Mrs. Carillon, a most important clue: *Noel never used a word longer than two syllables.* Do you understand what a help that is in solving the *glub-blubs*?" he asked the twins.

Tony shook his head. "They don't teach us syllables in school," he said, glad that it wasn't Mr. Banks he was telling this to.

"Let me try to explain. A syllable is the smallest unit of sound in a word. It is like a note in music—something you hear. You don't even have to know how to spell in order to count syllables; just say the word out loud, and you will hear them.

"Now, some words have only one syllable, like the word 'seek,' and the word 'seal.'

"Some words have two syllables, like 'ce-dar.'

"Some words have three syllables, like 'sea-son-al.' Is that clear?"

The twins nodded. They thought Augie Kunkel must be the smartest man in the world. So did Mrs. Carillon. She also thought he was rather good-looking in his football helmet; and that he must be quite fond of them, for he wasn't stuttering anymore.

"Since we know that Noel never used a word longer than two syllables in any of his other messages, we can presume that the same applies here. *The message contains only one-syllable or two-syllable words*."

The Three Unknowns

"Unfortunately, there are three things we don't know," Augie Kunkel continued.

"Remember, we are dealing with a spoken message, not a written one. Therefore:

We don't know how the sounds are spelled.

"For example: 'new' can be spelled nine different ways in one- and two-syllable words, and still sound the same.

> If 'new' is a word:
> > new
> > knew
> > gnu
> If 'new' is part of a word:
> > neu (neutral)
> > new (newsboy)
> > noe (canoe)
> > noo (noodle)
> > nou (nougat)
> > nu (nude)
> > nui (nuisance)."

"I saw a gnu in the zoo the other day," Mrs. Carillon said.

"A fascinating creature, the gnu."

"Please, Mr. Kunkel, go on about what we don't know," Tony pleaded.

****

"Mrs. Carillon heard sounds, not one-syllable words, or even complete syllables. Therefore:

We don't know where most words begin or end.

"For example: There are five possibilities for the 'C' sound:

'C____': the beginning of a word (season)
'____C': the end of a word (fancy)
'C': an initial (C.)
'C': one word (see, sea)
'C': part of a one-syllable word (seek)."

****

"Lastly, we can't be sure that 'new' is the final word or even part of the final word. Therefore:

We don't know where the message ends."

The Chart

"This is getting too complicated" Tony complained. He was beginning to wish that Mr. Kunkel wasn't quite so smart after all.

"I think this will make it easier." Augie Kunkel took another piece of paper from his pocket. "First let's write the message once again and number the syllables we are looking for."

Noel	____	C	____	all	I	____	new	. . .	} sounds
	1	2	3	4	5	6	7	?	} syllables

Noel___C___all

	1	2	1–2	2–3	3	3–4	4
Noel	___	C	___C	C___	___	___all	all
Noel		C.	fancy	season		local	all
Noel		see	gypsy	secret		candle	awl
Noel		sea		ceiling		nickel	ball
Noel		scene					halt

"That's all?" Tony said hopefully. "Just seven syllables?"

"Perhaps, but there may be several more after 'new.'"
Augie Kunkel drew lines on the paper dividing it into
columns which he headed and numbered. He wrote down
some words, then handed the paper to Tony.

"You* can begin by copying this chart on a large
sheet of ruled paper. All the possible combinations of
syllables are here, and I've suggested a few words for a
start. Once you and Tina have added as many words as
you can, we will cut the lists apart, matching them up
(1–2–3–4–5–6–7–?) without repeating any num-
bers, to see if we can arrange them into some meaning-
ful order."

"Can't we solve the *glub-blubs* without lists?" Tina
asked.

"Certainly, as long as you follow these three rules, for
the time being at least.

* You, too; but be sure to make your own chart. Penalty for writing
in this or any other book: six months in a pest-hole.

I_____new. . . .

5	6	5–6	6–7	7	7–?
I	——	I_____	——new	new	new. . . .
I		*island*	can*oe*	*new*	*new*sboy
eye		*ivy*	re*new*	*knew*	*nui*sance
my		*I*rish		*gnu*	*noo*dle
ice				*newt*	*New* Jersey

1. *Each sound is one syllable*
   or part of one syllable.
2. *No word is longer than two syllables."*

A waiter cleared his throat. They looked around, surprised to see they were the only diners left.

Augie Kunkel quickly paid the bill and escorted Mrs. Carillon and the twins home.

"And don't forget," he said as he left them at their door, "the most important rule of all:

3. *The message must make sense."*

Tony's List

Let's divide up the lists," Tony said after a sleepless night. "I'll take 'C' and you can have '_____C.' "

"Thanks a lot, you gave me the hardest one," Tina complained. "Just for that you can do the chart by yourself. I have my own plans."

"All right, you can have the 'C' list," Tony said. The school bell drowned out Tina's reply. The twins raced to their classroom, sat down at their desks, and began to write.

Tony wrote: "_____C."

Tina wrote: "Tony and I are a medical phenomenon!" She passed the note to Jordan Pinckney, who read it, shrugged, and tore it into little pieces.

Tina was furious with Jordan Pinckney. By the end of the day she was mad at the whole miserable world.

"You'd better pay more attention in class, Tony," she said, taking her anger out on the only person around, "or you're going to be kept back."

"Grea*sy*," Tony replied.

****

During the next few days Tony added "jui*cy*, i*cy*, spi*cy*" to the "_____C" list, and then he was stuck.

"Tina, you've got to help me. I've only got four words, so far; and Mr. Kunkel is coming over on Saturday."

"Don't worry," Tina said. "I've already solved the *glub-blubs*."

"Solved it?"

"That's right. You see, I've been working according to rule 3: *The message must make sense.* Well, the only thing that makes sense is that Noel is dead. In fact, he knew he was dying when he said:

> *See* you at my funer*al. I'*ve got *pneu*monia."

Tony shook his head. "Too many syllables."

"Well, if I were drowning I wouldn't pay any attention to syllables," Tina replied.

"Maybe *you* wouldn't, but you don't spell your name backward."

****

"Very c-c-clever," Augie Kunkel said, but Tina could tell from his stutter that he was afraid of hurting her feelings.

"Too many syllables, right, Mr. Kunkel?" Tony said.

"But it does make sense," Tina insisted.

"Not q-q-quite. You see, if Noel Carillon had pneumonia, the doctors would have kept him in the hospital after patching his elbow."

"Grea*sy*, jui*cy*, i*cy*, spi*cy*," Tony said and showed his chart to Augie Kunkel.

"Mercy."

"What's wrong?" Tony asked.

"N-n-nothing at all. I was just giving you more words for list 1–2: mer*cy*, sau*cy*, ra*cy*, la*cy*."

****

A week passed before Tony added his next word: "Sis*sy*." Augie Kunkel offered "*Tse-tse* fly." *

By this time the twins were barely speaking to each other, so Tony worked on the "C" list himself. "*Seam, sea*t, *cea*se," and one of his Spanish-speaking friends gave him the word for yes— "*Si.*"

"Excellent," Augie Kunkel remarked. "*Seize, siege, Si*kh."

"Wow!" Tony repeated the word "Sikh" three times. There was no doubt about it; Mr. Kunkel was surely the smartest man who ever lived, and Tony wanted to impress him. Not until he was well into the "C_____" list (*ce*dar, *see*saw, *se*nior, *sea*shore, *sea*side) did Tony real-

* A tricky one. Add "tse-tse" to list 1–2; and add "fly" to list 3.

ize that he was faced with a dilemma.

"What if I come up with the right answer to the *glub-blubs*?" Tony thought, and shuddered.

The fonder he became of Augie Kunkel, the less he wanted to find Noel Carillon.

Tina's Plan*

Tina believed in action, not list-making. She didn't bother telling the syllable-counters about her new solution:

See person*al* ad, *I*owa (or *I*daho) *new*spaper.

Every step was planned. Tina realized it would do no good looking up a personal ad placed more than twenty years ago; but someone who knew Noel might still be reading the same paper. She would place her own ads and pay for them with baby-sitting money.

Tina spent an afternoon in the library copying down names, addresses, and advertising rates of newspapers beginning with "Iowa" and "Idaho." Then she remembered there was something else she wanted to look up.

"Where are your medical books, please?"

The librarian recommended a biography of the doctors Mayo. It didn't contain the information Tina wanted, but she became so engrossed in the book that she had to be reminded of the late hour.

****

"Young lady, where have you been?" It was Mr. Banks again. "Mrs. Carillon has been beside herself with worry. And the fish is getting cold."

* There is a correct word in this section to add to the chart.

"Pork chops," said Tony.

Tina washed her hands quickly and sat down to dinner. Mr. Banks was explaining why he was moving to New York City.

"This family takes up so much of my time these days that all I do is travel back and forth. By the way, Mrs. Carillon, what are your plans for the summer?"

Tony choked on a piece of meat, and Mrs. Carillon whacked him on the back.

"That's what comes of gulping down food, young man," Mr. Banks said after the fuss was over. "I was asking about your summer plans. Not some wild-goose chase, I hope, or some expensive seaside resort?"

"I haven't given it much thought," Mrs. Carillon replied. She couldn't bring herself to think about leaving her seals.

Tony knew what they were going to do, but he wasn't going to tell Mr. Banks that they would remain in the city because he had to repeat history in summer school. He quickly changed the subject.

"Mr. Banks, can you think of a word beginning with a 'C' sound?"

"*C*.P.A. That means certified public accountant."

"What about a word ending in 'al'?"

"Leg*al*," answered Mr. Banks.

"How do you spell it?"

"Young man, what *do* they teach you in that school?"

"How about 'I'?"

"You should say: 'How about me?' What do they teach. . . ?"

"What word can you think of with a 'new' sound in it?"

Mr. Banks, for once, didn't mind being interrupted. He

enjoyed showing off his quick wit. "Internal Reve*nue* Service," he answered. "That's the income tax bureau."

Tony shook his head over the excess of syllables, but Tina thought Mr. Banks proved his point well. If Noel's message was about money, then surely he must be dead.

"Another pork chop, Tony?" Mrs. Carillon asked.

"What's for dessert?"

"Camembert cheese."

"Another pork chop, please."

Mrs. Carillon looked at her watch. "Good heavens, I've almost missed the racing results."

"Racing results?" shouted the horrified Mr. Banks. "Have you taken up gambling on top of everything else?"

Mrs. Carillon, transistor radio to her ear, didn't hear the question. Tina allayed Mr. Banks' fear.

"She doesn't gamble. She just loves the horse Christmas Bells and Seymour. . ."

"He won! He won!" Mrs. Carillon turned off the radio, all smiles. "Mark my word, Christmas Bells is a shoo-in to win the Triple Crown."

Summer in New York

Christmas Bells won the Triple Crown.

The sea lions in Central Park grew so fat their keeper had to eliminate regular feedings.

Tina became the busiest baby-sitter in the building. Although too absorbed in her books to keep a close eye on the accident-prone children, she disinfected their wounds and applied gauze and tape bandages with a near professional skill.

Most of all, Tina enjoyed sitting with the Stein baby. The infant slept throughout the evening, and Dr. Stein never locked his bookcases. Tina had difficulty with the technical language in the medical books, but she was fascinated by the gory pictures and case histories. She even collected some words for Tony's chart: *ce*cum and *se*cretion,* hospit*al** and spin*al,* *i*odine* and *i*sotope,* *neu*trophil* and *nu*cleus.*

By the end of August Tina had earned enough money to place an ad in every Iowa and Idaho newspaper on her list.

> WANTED: INFORMATION ON WHEREABOUTS OF NOEL CARILLON. WIFE DESPERATE. REWARD!! WRITE TINA CARILLON 802 PARK AVE. N.Y. N.Y.

Tina had no reward money. She would leave that up to Mr. Banks, when the time came.

****

Tina worried about Mr. Banks and his frequent visits. He was their dinner guest two to three times a week, and he always had papers to be signed. Maybe he was cheating Mrs. Carillon out of her share of the soup business. Maybe he was planning to marry her for her money. On the other hand, Mr. Banks was so stingy that maybe he just wanted a free meal.

"How can you stand him?" Tina would ask every time Mr. Banks created a scene.

Mrs. Carillon's answer was always the same. "He really is a very nice man. He just frets over us so much that it upsets him."

Tony preferred the company of Mr. Kunkel, and he knew that Mrs. Carillon did, too. She smiled a lot when he was around. Tuesdays and Saturdays were Augie Kun-

* "Too many syllables," Tony said.

kel nights; and Tony was always prepared with a few more words for his chart.

"List 3–4: ov*al*, snowb*all*, sand*al*, scand*al*."

"Cymb*al*," said Augie Kunkel.

"List 4: c*all*, h*all*, squ*all*," said Tony. "List 5: m*i*ne, n*i*ne, w*i*ne."

"I thought of 'hall' twenty years ago," Mrs. Carillon said. "But 'wine' is a good word. Noel was so genteel."

Tony added word after word, following Mr. Kunkel's rules to the letter, except rule 3. He didn't want the message to make sense. Whenever Augie Kunkel suggested they cut the lists apart and match them up, Tony insisted that he hadn't quite finished. The closest he came to putting words together in a logical order was "The *sea* is s*al*t."

Tina was the rule 3 believer in the family. She told no one about her newspaper ads, but she did need help in carrying out another idea.

"I know it has too many syllables, but it does make sense," she argued. "The reason Noel left Palm Beach was that he had to get back to work. He worked on a ship that was sailing the next day. The only place Mrs. Carillon would be able to locate him was through his job registration:

Noel Carillon, *Sea*man's Hiring H*all*, *New* York."

Augie Kunkel said that Tina's reasoning was so good he wouldn't count syllables. In fact he would go to the National Maritime Union Hiring Hall, himself.

Tony thought it was a terrible idea. "Some seaman. His boat capsizes five minutes after it hits water."

Tony was right; it was a terrible idea. Not only was no Noel Carillon registered with the union, but several seamen took a violent dislike to snooping. The cry of "Fink!" spread through the hiring hall, and Augie Kunkel was lucky to escape with no more than a bloody nose and a sprained ankle, thanks to the football helmet.

Tina made no suggestions after that. She still had her newspaper ads; and if that didn't work out, she would do what she knew Mr. Kunkel had decided to do: wait. Wait for new evidence to turn up, or wait for Mrs. Carillon to admit that Noel was dead.

Just wait.

Tony Makes a Discovery

It was a time of waiting for everyone.

Mrs. Carillon was waiting for Christmas Bells to win the Washington Park Handicap.

Tina was waiting for letters from Iowa and Idaho; and she was waiting for school to begin. She had decided to confess to Jordan Pinckney that she was not a Siamese twin. Then, if he would admit that his father was not a television star, they could become friends.

Tony was waiting for Augie Kunkel to return from a two-week visit to his Aunt Martha. He had not been able to think of a new word for his chart since the end of summer school. In desperation, he asked Mrs. Carillon to show him the original anniversary cards from Noel.

She obviously hadn't looked at them in quite some time, Tony noted approvingly, as he blew away the dust, untied the purple ribbon, and carefully removed each card from its envelope. He examined them front and back, inside and out. Mrs. Carillon's memory was faultless; he didn't find one new word.

Then his eye fell on the return name and address on one of the envelopes. There was one of his list words—and a new word. Mrs. Carillon had never mentioned what was written on the envelopes. He looked at the others; they were all the same. Suddenly, Tony realized why the two words sounded so familiar. He had the answer! He had solved the first part of the *glub-blubs!* If only Mr. Kunkel would hurry back so he could tell him the news.

In his excitement, Tony overlooked the consequence of his discovery:

HE HAD FOUND NOEL CARILLON.

Missing Minnie

"I spend all afternoon cooking, and all you do is pick."

"I'm not very hungry, Mrs. Baker," Tony replied.

"None of you seem hungry. What a waste!"

Tina whispered to Tony that Mrs. Baker sounded just like Mr. Banks. She was overheard.

"And what's wrong with sounding like Mr. Banks? He's the only one who makes any sense around here. Such a fine, upstanding man, and handsome, too. If I were you, Mrs. Carillon, I wouldn't miss an opportunity like that. I'd latch on to Mr. Banks without a second's thought."

"Why, what do you mean, Mrs. Baker?"

"Marriage, Mrs. Carillon, that's what I mean. Marriage. A husband for you and a father for your children."

"Mr. Banks for a father?" Tony was horrified.

"Ugh!" groaned Tina.

"But I am married, Mrs. Baker."

"It's time you forgot about that Noel. As Mr. Banks says, he's legally good as dead. You're lonely, and the twins are lonely, and I know."

The twins looked at each other in surprise. They didn't think they were lonely. Mrs. Carillon didn't think she was lonely, either. It must be Mrs. Baker who was lonely.

"You must miss your husband very much since he died," Mrs. Carillon said.

"Miss that good-for-nothing? Not him. Spend money, that's all he knew how to do. I'd make money and he'd spend it." Mrs. Baker sighed and sat down, dish towel in hand. "But I sure do miss my sister Minnie." *

"What happened to Minnie?" Tina asked, hoping for a detailed medical case history.

"Don't rightly know. I sent her bus fare to come to New York over six months ago, and I haven't heard from her since. And nobody back home in Davenport knows anything, either."

"How dreadful," said Mrs. Carillon.

"Do we have to have Camembert cheese every night?" complained Tony.

Letters from Iowa and Idaho

Tony spent the opening day of school writing Noel's first phrase over and over. When class was dismissed early, he went home and wrote it some more. He had one more day of waiting for Mr. Kunkel's return.

This was Tina's big day. Jordan Pinckney had grown three inches over the summer and was the tallest boy in the class. And the handsomest, she thought. Tina cornered him after school and made her confession. Jordan Pinckney said he knew it all along; and, even worse, still insisted his father was a television star. "If you don't believe me watch Channel 2 at 7:30 tonight."

"Don't worry, I will," she said, and walked part of the way home with Rosemary Neuberger.

* Minnie who?

"You know, Rosemary, since you got pimples you've become a much nicer person."

Rosemary Neuberger had become such a nice person, she didn't even object to Tina's free medical advice.

"Remember, now, lots of soap and no chocolate."

****

Ten letters addressed to Tina Carillon were stacked on the hall table.

"Pen pals," she explained to her nosy brother.

Tina neatly arranged the envelopes on her bedspread and studied them appreciatively. She wanted to savor every precious moment leading to the final discovery. Slowly, carefully, she opened the first letter; then stopped. What if she and Mr. Banks were wrong? What if one of the letters said that Noel Carillon was alive and well and living in Idaho? For several minutes she considered tossing them down the incinerator, but curiosity won out and she unfolded the letter.

> *No need to be lonely! Our computers can match you to the partner you have always dreamed of. Our introductory offer of 3 names for only $10. . .*

The next letter promised popularity through weight reduction: Enroll in SYLPH; the Suddenly-You-Lose-Pounds-Happily club of northern Iowa.

Two letters touted the services of private detectives: one from Idaho at $50 a day, one from Iowa at $75.*

For $5 she could have her personal astrological horoscope cast by experts; for $7.50 she could buy a tonic to cure her "tired" blood.

---

* There are more people to investigate in Iowa.

She was invited to join a lonely hearts' club, offered a combination accident-health-life insurance policy "for the single woman," and guaranteed satisfaction for one year with the purchase of a reconditioned vacuum cleaner.

The last envelope, written in an almost illegible scrawl, contained five pages of mad ravings and obscene proposals. Tina had read enough medical case histories not to be too upset by it; she figured the miserable writer was either suffering from brain damage or a fatal kidney disease. She tore up the letter and threw it into the waste-paper basket, along with the others.

"Maybe Jordan Pinckney's father really is a television star," she thought, trying to rouse herself from a gnawing sense of despair.

Who's Minnie Baker?

Tina and Tony were edgy enough without having Mr. Banks show up for dinner; but there he was again with papers to be signed.

"Fish!" he exclaimed when Mrs. Baker brought the stuffed bass to the table. He had begun to suspect his sense of smell; but, for once, he had guessed correctly.

Tony lost his appetite thinking about the possibility of Mrs. Carillon marrying Mr. Banks. Besides, he hated fish even more than Camembert cheese.

Tina couldn't eat, either.

"Young lady, why do you keep looking at your watch?"

"Jordan Pinckney's father is supposed to be on television at 7:30."

"Pinky?" screamed Mrs. Carillon, jumping up from her chair. "Pinky?"

"I said *Pinck*ney. Jordan Pinckney——he's a boy in my

class." Tina was rather interested in the understandable mistake. She wondered how old Jordan's father was.

Mrs. Carillon, embarrassed by her outburst, sat down and smiled sheepishly, as Mrs. Baker tsk-tsked her way back to the kitchen.

"Poor Mrs. Baker," Mrs. Carillon said quickly, before Mr. Banks could begin his lecture. "Did you know that her sister has been missing for the past six months?"

The twins expected Mr. Banks to say: "Not another missing person!" but he seemed truly sorry to hear the sad news.

"What a pity," he said. "Perhaps I can take steps to locate her." He saw the twins' surprised expressions and explained, "Mrs. Baker works hard for this family; and good cooks are hard to find."

"What is her sister's name?" he asked Mrs. Carillon.

"Minnie. Minnie Baker, I guess."

"Who's Minnie Baker?" Mrs. Baker asked, returning with a bowl of mashed potatoes.

"Why, your missing sister," Mrs. Carillon replied.

"My missing sister is *my* sister, not my dead husband's." Mrs. Baker placed the potatoes in front of Tony. "Her name is Potts. Mineola Potts."

"Mineola Potts!" screamed Mrs. Carillon, jumping up from her chair again. "Mineola Potts! Why that was the name of my cellmate in the Women's House of Detention."

Tony stuffed himself with mashed potatoes; and Tina stared at her watch, while Mrs. Baker and Mrs. Carillon "couldn't get over the coincidence."

Mr. Banks assured the women that he would look into the matter first thing in the morning. He finished his plate of cheese and fruit, and left at 7:25.

*The Third Scream**

A cereal commercial, a cleanser commercial, station identification, then: *Marshal from Montana.*

"That's funny," said Mrs. Carillon, "I can't remember having been in Montana."

Starring Bryan Fink and Hardy Hamburger.

"I told you Jordan Pinckney was a liar," Tony said.

"Maybe he changed his name," replied Tina. "Lots of actors do."

"To Fink or Hamburger?"

Tonight's Special Guest Star: Newton Pinckney.

"There, see," Tina said excitedly.

A gasoline commercial, a toothpaste commercial, and *Marshal from Montana* began.

"Wonderful, a cowboy show." Mrs. Carillon clapped her hands with delight as three bandits, hidden high among the boulders, mounted their skittish horses.

Tina wondered which one was Newton Pinckney.

The tall bandit pulled down the kerchief that was concealing his face in order to speak. "The stagecoach should be coming 'round the bend any minute now. Let's go!"

For the third time that evening Mrs. Carillon jumped up from her seat.

"Leon, Noel," she screamed, and fainted.

****

Tony ran to answer the telephone, thinking the problem was her painful right arm. Mrs. Baker dashed out from the kitchen with a glass of water. Tina knelt on the floor and felt Mrs. Carillon's pulse.

* And the unheard sounds . . . .

"Nothing to worry about," Tina announced, wishing she had a wristwatch with a second hand, "but as long as you're at the telephone, Tony, why don't you call Dr. Stein."

Tina described her discovery to Dr. Stein. "It's a new disease, unknown to medical history, which I call 'the jumping-up-from-the-chair-and-screaming syndrome.'"

Dr. Stein called it nerves. He prescribed a mild sedative and told Mrs. Carillon to rest in bed for the next few days.

****

Mrs. Carillon slept peacefully through the night. No one else in the household did.

Tina lay awake trying to figure out the Pinky-Pinckney relationship.

Tony lay awake fidgeting. Waiting for Mr. Kunkel's return had become unbearable. He was tempted to take one of Mrs. Carillon's pills but was afraid it might contain something for women only.

Mrs. Baker was the one who most needed the pill, but she believed that the best medicine was a well-balanced diet. She lay awake picturing her poor sister Minnie locked up in what Tina so luridly described as the "pest-hole."

Mrs. Carillon slept through the morning. Mrs. Baker couldn't remember if she had made breakfast; and the twins couldn't remember if they had eaten any.

It was going to be a long day.

The Long Day

"I saw your father on television last night. You look just like him," Tina said, fishing for a clue.

"So they say."

Tina studied Jordan Pinckney as he walked away. Tall, thin, handsome; his father must have been the character who pulled down his kerchief and said, "Let's go." That was when Mrs. Carillon fainted.

Tina suddenly remembered that Mrs. Carillon was confined to bed. She stopped at a newsstand to buy her a magazine with a picture of Christmas Bells on the cover. Tony hadn't forgotten, either. He brought home a library book about seals.

"How thoughtful," Mrs. Carillon said, wondering why the pictures in the book didn't look like the seals she knew. "Now that I've got plenty to keep me busy, why don't you two go help Mrs. Baker. She's so jittery, today."

"*She's* jittery!" Tony said, but went into the kitchen, anyway. Tina went to her room; she had more thinking to do about Pinky-Pinckney.

****

"Tony, I've been trying to reach Mr. Banks all day," Mrs. Baker said, twisting and untwisting the potholder in her hands. "Would you do me a favor and call him for me? I'm so nervous."

"*You're* nervous!" Tony said.

Mr. Banks had just returned from the Women's House of Detention. Mineola Potts was, indeed, there. He had arranged for Mrs. Baker to visit her tomorrow morning at nine o'clock.

"What a kind man," Mrs. Baker said when Tony finished his report of the phone call.

"Ugh!" said Tony.

****

"Is Mr. Kunkel here yet?" Tina appeared in the dining room just as Tony finished setting the table. "I've got something terribly important to tell him."

"*You've* got something to tell him!"

"How do I look?" asked Mrs. Carillon. She was wearing a purple-flowered hostess gown.

"Like the sofa," Mrs. Baker said. "It's a good thing Mr. Banks isn't here to see you looking like that."

"I think you look smashing," said Tina.

"B-b-beautiful," said Augie Kunkel when Mrs. Carillon opened the door. He was so overwhelmed by the warm welcome that he was stuttering again. It hardly mattered, for everyone was talking at the same time.

"Mr. Kunkel, I have something to tell you. . ."

". . .Mineola Potts. . ."

". . .something terribly important. . ."

". . .and I fainted dead away."

". . .the first part of the *glub-blubs*. . ."

". . .Christmas Bells. . ."

"Did someone say Christmas B-B-Bells?"

"I did," Mrs. Carillon replied. "Christmas Bells is the horse that. . ."

"Yes, I know. Strange, I n-n-never noticed the c-c-coincidence." Augie Kunkel paused to control his stammer. "You see, the French word for Christmas is 'Noel,' and 'Carillon' means 'bells.' "

"You mean Christmas Bells means Noel Carillon?" Mrs. Carillon said. "No wonder I like that horse."

Tony knew that it was more than a coincidence. "Mr. Kunkel, I've just got to talk to you—alone. Please."

"I have to talk to you, too, Mr. Kunkel," Tina said. "In private. It's terribly important."

Mrs. Baker emerged from the kitchen. "If you two

talked to each other for a change, instead of always arguing, you wouldn't be bothered with so many secrets. Besides, dinner's ready."

****

Mrs. Carillon talked of horses; Augie Kunkel described in detail how his Aunt Martha was fighting a losing battle with termites and dry rot; and the twins sulked. The evening was almost over.

"B-b-but the garden is lovely now; abloom with white clematis (*C. paniculata*), autumn crocus (*Colchicum*), and fleece-vine (*Polygonum auberti*)."

Mrs. Carillon stifled a yawn. Augie Kunkel rose, invited them to dinner on Saturday, and bid them goodnight.

Part One of the Glub-blubs

Saturday was too far off. The twins decided they had to
see Mr. Kunkel early the next morning (or, as Tina put
it, they would die of hypertension). That meant skipping
school, but Tina thought of a good excuse. It was Rosh
Hashanah. "After all, we *are* orphans," she said, "so we
could be Jewish as far as anyone knows."

Although they walked together across the park, the
twins still had not told one another about their discover-
ies. "That would be going too far," thought Tony.

Augie Kunkel had never invited Mrs. Carillon or the
twins to his apartment. He wasn't especially ashamed of
his fourth-floor walk-up with its shabby furniture; there
was just no place to sit. Books were everywhere: on the
chairs, on his desk, on the floor, on the sink.

Tony, knowing his friend would be flustered by their
unexpected arrival, had written down his discovery in
order to save time and embarrassment. He handed the
note to Mr. Kunkel before he was able to stammer out a
greeting.

Augie Kunkel was even more bewildered after reading
Tony's message. He sat down on the one empty chair and
read aloud:

Noel _____ C _____ all = *Noel* is *Sey*mour H*all*.

"Who is Seymour Hall?" he asked.

"Seymour Hall is the name of the jockey who owns Christmas Bells. Noel Carillon and Seymour Hall are one and the same person. That's why Mrs. Carillon is so taken with him; somewhere, down deep, she recognizes the little boy she married."

Tony expected Tina to object; surprisingly enough, she didn't.

It was Augie Kunkel who was being difficult.

"What you say, Tony, is quite ingenious; but let's go over the facts:

   1. The syllables fit perfectly.

   2. Mrs. Carillon does seem unusually obsessed with the jockey Seymour Hall and his horse.

   3. Christmas Bells does mean Noel Carillon.

"But does it really make sense? Can we answer these questions:

   1. Why did Noel Carillon change his name again?

   2. Why did he choose the name Seymour Hall?

   3. If Noel Carillon is Seymour Hall, who was the man in the boat?"

"I can answer the second question," Tony said. "Noel Carillon chose the name Seymour Hall because that was the name of his school. It was on the envelopes of all the anniversary cards."

"And I can answer the third question," Tina said. "I know who the man in the boat was!"

Part Two of the Glub-blubs

Tina wrote her solution under Tony's.

I _____ new. . . . = *I* am *New*ton Pinckney.

"Who is Newton Pinckney?" Mr. Kunkel asked.

"Newton Pinckney is a tall, thin, handsome actor about forty-some years old. When Mrs. Carillon saw him on television, she screamed and fainted. It was such a shock that she blotted it out of her mind completely. My guess is that Newton Pinckney was Noel Carillon's friend, the one he called 'Pinky.' He was the man in the boat."

"Hmmm," pondered Augie Kunkel. "*Noel is Seymour Hall; I am Newton Pinckney.* But why? Why did Noel change his name?"

"To avoid Mrs. Carillon," said Tony.

"Why did Newton Pinckney confess?"

"Because he thought he was drowning," said Tina.

"But why, why? Why all the pretense and false identities? How long was it supposed to last?"

"Maybe Newton Pinckney was supposed to kill Mrs. Carillon, so he and Noel could split the inheritance," suggested Tony.

"That's impossible," Tina shouted; but she wasn't too sure. Jordan's father did play a convincing crook.

"Not intentional murder, oh no, I can't believe that," Augie Kunkel said. "After all, Noel had a fortune of his own which he has never laid claim to. But I do admit there is something very strange here. I suggest we verify a few facts before we tell Mrs. Carillon."

"Tell Mrs. Carillon?" gasped Tony. "Do we have to tell her? I don't want a jockey for a father."

"When the time comes we will have to tell her the truth," Augie Kunkel said, sadly.

The Verifiers

They called themselves The Verifiers.

> Motto: Find the facts.
> Meetings: Every other Thursday afternoon, after school.
> Place: Mr. Kunkel's apartment.
> Agenda: Present evidence.
> Discuss strategy.
> Chocolate cake and milk.

Tony liked the cake and milk idea; but he wasn't so sure he wanted to find the facts. Tina argued that once Mrs. Carillon learned the truth she would divorce Noel and marry Mr. Kunkel.* That was enough to convince Tony to cull old sports magazines and newspaper files for facts about Seymour Hall. He read his report at the second meeting of The Verifiers.

> *Seymour Hall is known as the "Mystery Rider" because nothing is known about his early life. He won his first race as an apprentice jockey in Florida twenty-one-years ago. He was one of the best jockeys in the country and retired, a rich man, five years ago. A few years later he bought a horse and named it Christmas Bells. Nobody could get that horse to*

* Or Mr. Banks, Tina thought, but kept that miserable idea to herself.

run, except Seymour Hall; so he became a jockey again. He and Christmas Bells have never lost a race.

Seymour Hall never married, but there are many pictures of him with beautiful women—all blondes.

"Well, we can at least tell Mrs. Carillon to stop having her hair dyed black," Tina said. Her only fact for the day was that Newton Pinckney had a scar on his right elbow.

Augie Kunkel reported on his visit to the Seymour Hall Boarding School for Boys. Newton Pinckney had, indeed, been a classmate of Leon Carillon. He showed the graduation picture of Leon (Noel) Carillon to Tony.

"That's him. That's Seymour Hall."

He showed the picture of Newton (Pinky) Pinckney to Tina, who nodded her approval; although she thought it looked more like Jordan than his father.

The vote to verify: *Noel is Seymour Hall; I am Newton Pinckney* was unanimous.

"Do we have to tell Mrs. Carillon now?" Tony asked.

"Not yet," Mr. Kunkel replied. "Not until we know 'why?' "

The Investigators

The Verifiers changed their name to The Investigators.

> Motto: Why?
> Meetings: Same time, same place.
> Agenda: Present evidence.
> > Discuss strategy.
> > Angel Food cake* and milk.

* Rosemary Neuberger wasn't the only one prone to pimples.

Augie Kunkel urged the utmost caution in their investigations. After all, they didn't want to frighten Newton Pinckney or Seymour Hall with criminal accusations.

"Maybe just a pleasant letter would do," he suggested.

"Actors never read their mail," Tina said. "I'll have to see Newton Pinckney in person."

"That may be a good idea," Mr. Kunkel replied, "but jockeys read their mail; I'm sure they do."

A LETTER TO SEYMOUR HALL

Dear Mr. Hall:

Please do not panic, but read this letter to the end. I mean you no harm and promise not to reveal your secret to the public.

You probably don't remember me after all these years, but we played together as children. I am the chubby boy who lived up the road—Augie Kunkel. My father was factory foreman.

I am in possession of incontrovertible evidence that you are Leon (Noel) Carillon, the husband of my dear friend Mrs. Carillon, who has not, as yet, been informed of your identity. She has kept a faithful vigil for you these many years, and deserves an explanation regarding your desertion.

If you do not plan to resume your role as husband to this good woman, some suitable action should be taken (agreeable to both parties) that will allow her to pursue a life of her own.

Please write to me, not to Mrs. Carillon, so I may present her with the truth as gently as possible.

Your friend,
Augie Kunkel

ANOTHER LETTER TO SEYMOUR HALL

Dear Mr. Hall:

You don't know me, but I know all about you. You are not the Mystery Rider called Seymour Hall. You are my father Noel Carillon, and I am your adopted son Tony.

I know you don't want a son; and I want Mr. Kunkel to be my father. So please divorce Mrs. Carillon. Mr. Banks will give you half of the Pomato Soup money.

Yours truly,
Tony Carillon

P.S. You also have an adopted daughter Tina, who is miserable.

****

Tina tried everything short of blackmail to persuade Jordan Pinckney to arrange a private interview for her with his father.

"If everyone who wanted to see my father in person saw my father in person, he wouldn't have any time left to act."

Two weeks passed.

No one had any "Why's" to report at the next meeting of The Investigators. Tony suggested changing their motto to "Wait," but Mr. Kunkel thought "Persevere" was a better word.

Tina persevered. One week later, after convincing him that it was a matter of life and death and promising to do his math homework for a month, Jordan Pinckney handed Tina's note to his father.

Dear Pinky:

"NOEL IS SEYMOUR HALL; I AM NEWTON PINCKNEY."
I can't say anymore because I know your son will read
this. If this message interests you, I am waiting outside
your front door ready to talk.

Tina Carillon

Tina didn't have long to wait. A look of utter astonish-
ment masked Jordan's face when he opened the door.

"My father wants to see you."

Does She Know?

Everything happened at once. Augie Kunkel and Tony
received replies from Seymour Hall the same afternoon
that Tina talked to Newton Pinckney.

Tony was reading the jockey's letter for the tenth time
when he heard the familiar scream. He ran into the living
room, straight into Mrs. Baker who spilled a glass of
water on Mr. Banks who was fanning Mrs. Carillon with
a newspaper. Mrs. Carillon was slumped across the
couch in a dead faint.

"What happened?" Tina asked as she hurried over to
Mrs. Carillon and began massaging her wrists. "Does she
know?"

"No," said Tony, picking himself up off the floor.

"Yes," said Mr. Banks, drying his face.

Mrs. Baker ran from the kitchen with more water and
bumped into Augie Kunkel, who had just come in the
open door.

"What happened?" Mr. Kunkel asked as he rushed
over to the prone Mrs. Carillon, water dripping down his
cheeks. "Does she know?"

"No," said Tony.

"Yes," said Mr. Banks.

"Somebody get some water," Tina shouted.

Just then Mrs. Carillon opened her eyes. The sight of Augie Kunkel and Mr. Banks with handkerchiefs to their faces brought back the bad news. She sat up slowly and turned to the twins. "He's dead," she said softly.

Tina and Mr. Kunkel were confused; only Tony understood. He broke into loud sobs and threw himself into the arms of Mrs. Carillon. They cried together.

"Who's d-d-dead?" whispered Augie Kunkel.

"No one we know," answered Mr. Banks and read aloud from the wet newspaper.

JOCKEY KILLED IN SPILL; HORSE O.K.

Seymour Hall, owner-jockey of Triple Crown winner Christmas Bells, was killed instantly in a freak accident during prerace warm-ups at Aqueduct today. The exact cause of the fatal fall from his horse is still unknown, but eyewitness accounts agree that the jockey, not the horse, became unusually distressed when the band struck up a tune.* It appeared that Seymour Hall threw his hands up to his ears to block out the sound of the music. The sudden jerk on the reins. . .

"Does anybody around here want dinner?" asked Mrs. Baker.

"Good idea," replied Mr. Banks, folding the newspaper. "That should cheer us all up. It's too bad about that jockey; but, after all, he wasn't a member of the family."

"Yes, he was!" cried Tony.

* "On Wisconsin."

Time for the Truth

"Let me t-t-tell you about Seymour Hall," Augie Kunkel said to the bewildered Mrs. Carillon.

"What about dinner?" complained Mr. Banks.

"Dinner can wait!" Augie Kunkel surprised everyone with his new-found authority. He stood in the middle of the room waiting for quiet.

"The death of the jockey, Seymour Hall, is a tragic loss to all of us," he began. He spoke slowly, deliberating over each word in an effort to control his stammer.

"Seymour Hall was a good man. He had much success in his lifetime, and much sadness."

Mrs. Carillon was kneading a tightly balled handkerchief in her hands. Augie Kunkel wasn't sure she was listening. "This most tragic accident, Mrs. Carillon, comes at a time. . ."

"If you have something to say, get on with it," Mr. Banks said. He was comfortably seated in a wing chair, munching on the Camembert cheese and crackers Mrs. Baker had set beside him.

Tony glowered at Mr. Banks, but Augie Kunkel knew he was right. He drew a chair up to the couch and sat down facing Mrs. Carillon.

"Mrs. Carillon, I have a letter for you that arrived only this morning. It will explain everything."

Mrs. Carillon took the letter in her trembling hand and looked around her, at inquisitive Tina leaning against Augie Kunkel's chair, at sad Tony slumped down next to her, at Mr. Banks munching and crunching away.

"Tina, would you read this aloud, please?"

Tina took the letter and cleared her throat.

Dear Mrs. Carillon:

I have never been good with words; but I will try to explain things. I hope that some day you will be able to forgive me.

"Who's the letter from?" Mrs. Carillon asked anxiously. "Quick, Tina, look at the bottom. Is it from Leon?"

"It's signed: *Noel (Seymour Hall)*."

"What?" shouted Mr. Banks, nearly choking on a cracker. "Go on, Tina," Augie Kunkel said.

You see, I didn't know you were waiting for me all these years. I thought Pinky had told you that I had gone away and not to look for me when you saw him on the dock in Palm Beach.

"That was Pinky in the boat," mumbled Mrs. Carillon. She shook her head over the folly of her long search.

Please believe me, I was not running away from you. I was running away from the soup business and all it stood for.

"That's what's wrong with this younger generation," Mr. Banks complained. "No sense of responsibility."

I changed my name and began a new life as a jockey. I wanted to tell you all this myself, but at the last minute I lost my nerve and asked my friend Pinky to explain. I guess I was worried that you might make me change my mind.

I almost did change my mind when you hugged me on the dock. . .

"I remember now. No wonder Seymour Hall looked so

familiar," Mrs. Carillon said with a wan smile. "I ran up to Leon and hugged him—then some pretty blonde woman dragged him away."

. . .but Alice or Doris or someone dragged me away. I left on the next plane and never saw Pinky again. Many times I've wished that I had talked to you, but I won't complain. I've had a good career and have been happy with horses.

If Mr. Banks is still around. . .

"What does he mean, if I'm still around?"

. . .tell him to give you my share of the soup money.

> *Love,*
> *Noel (Seymour Hall)*

P.S. You are lucky to have a good friend like Augie.

Everyone, including Dr. Stein, whom Mrs. Baker had called (just in case), was waiting for Mrs. Carillon to jump up and scream, or faint; but she just sat there, her purple flowers fading into the purple-flowered couch.

More of the Truth

"I have another letter to read." All heads turned from Mrs. Carillon back to Tina. "It's from Pinky."

My dear Mrs. Carillon:

Your lovely daughter Tina. . .

"I don't believe it," said Tony. "Show me the letter."
"Newton Pinckney is that actor we saw on television,

Mrs. Carillon," Tina explained while Tony examined the handwriting to make sure it wasn't his sister's.

Tina began again.

Your lovely daughter Tina has just told me how badly I bungled my role in our little drama. It never occurred to me that you didn't hear all the words of what I thought was my dying confession: "Noel is Seymour Hall; I am Newton Pinckney."

"Noel *glub* C *blub* all. . .I *glub* new. . . ." Mrs. Carillon repeated.

"Never could understand those method actors," complained Mr. Banks.

Noel was a very mixed-up character who felt he could only bring you unhappiness. He was going to ask you to forget he ever existed; but, at the last moment, he came down with a bad case of stage fright. That's when I entered the picture.

I'm afraid it was a poor job of casting; the role was much too difficult for an inexperienced actor. As soon as the curtain went up, I forgot my lines (that's why I let you think I was Noel).

I proceeded to botch up one scene after another, and before the last act was over, I ran.

That, Mrs. Carillon, was the worst performance of my life. You will be happy to learn that my acting has greatly improved since then.

> *Best wishes,*
> *Newton Pinckney*

"Newton Pinckney is a ham," said Tony.

A Gift Horse

"Well, that seems to clear things up, except for my job,"
Mr. Banks rose from his chair to go to the dinner table.
"I'm going to have plenty of work straightening up that
estate. Why, the horse alone is worth. . ."

"I have a letter, too," said Tony.

"Another letter!" Mr. Banks sat down again.

Mrs. Carillon was the only one not taken by surprise.
She gave an almost imperceptible nod, and Tony began
to read.

Dear Tony:

*I am sorry that I don't know you, for you sound like a
son I'd be proud to have. . .*

"Let me see that," Tina said. This time Tony had to
wait for Tina to compare the handwriting with Augie
Kunkel's letter before he could continue.

*. . .but I'm afraid it's too late to start being a father.
Augie Kunkel will take better care of you, Tina, and
Mrs. Carillon than I could ever hope to do.*

"Augie Kunkel!" shouted Mr. Banks. "I'm the one
who's been looking after this family."

Augie Kunkel turned a deep red. Tony quickly re-
sumed reading.

*I do have a son of sorts: Christmas Bells. He is a great
horse with a most gentle nature. I will race him one more
time, then send him to a farm near-by where you can visit*

him. He deserves the pleasures of the pasture and should make a fine stud.

I've been feeling poorly of late and have to go away for a long rest. Christmas Bells is the one thing in the world I love and the only thing I have to offer. He belongs to you and Tina now.

"Christmas Bells!" Tina shrieked with delight. "Did you hear that, Mrs. Carillon, Christmas Bells!"

Mrs. Carillon's lips moved to form the words "Christmas Bells" but no sound came out. She rose slowly, walked to her bedroom, and closed the door behind her.

"She'll get over it," Dr. Stein said. "Just leave her be."

Leave Her Be

Days went by when Mrs. Carillon didn't utter one word. She barely ate and scarcely slept; her purple-flowered dresses sagged where once they were snug; and an inch of gray rimmed the roots of her hair.

Augie Kunkel took her to the zoo, but she wasn't interested in feeding what he called "sea lions." Mr. Banks, to everyone's surprise, suggested she buy some new clothes; but she wasn't interested in shopping. Even stories about Christmas Bells fell on deaf ears.

"She'll get over it; just leave her be," Dr. Stein said every time Tina consulted him on Mrs. Carillon's condition, and lingered to thumb through his books.

So they let her be, and waited; and finally it happened.

****

It was a month to the day of Noel's death. Augie Kunkel was there for dinner, and Mr. Banks (as usual). Tina and Tony were talking about visiting Christmas Bells in December.

"Christmas Bells?" Mrs. Carillon mumbled, trying to remember where she had heard that name before.

"That horse had better make a good stud. Why, you wouldn't believe what it costs. . ."

Mrs. Baker set the roast duck on the table with a disapproving thud, and Mr. Banks switched to a more pleasant subject.

"By the way, Mrs. Carillon, I do have a bit of good news. Mineola Potts will be paroled soon, now that I've found her a job."

"Did you hear that, Mrs. Carillon," Tina said. "Mineola Potts is getting out of jail."

"Mineola Potts?" Mrs. Carillon looked puzzled.

"I have good news, too; though not as good as Mr. Banks'," Augie Kunkel said modestly. "I've won third prize* for inventing the most difficult crossword puzzle."

"Great!" Tony exclaimed. "Did you hear that, Mrs. Carillon? Mr. Kunkel won a prize."

"That's nice," Mrs. Carillon said, to everyone's relief. At least she hadn't asked who Mr. Kunkel was.

"Crossword puzzles," remarked Mr. Banks. "Now that might be a nice profession for you, Tina."

"I'm going to be a doctor."

"In case you've forgotten, young lady, you're a girl. Now, maybe a nurse. . ."

"I'm going to be a doctor!"

"Veterinary, now there's a profession. If you saw the bills from that horse doctor. . ."

Tony sensed that Mr. Banks was going to question him next. He tried to decide quickly what he wanted to be, but couldn't make up his mind.

"I'm going to be a real doctor!" Tina insisted.

Mr. Banks shook his head and turned to Tony.

Tony still hadn't made up his mind. All he could think of was sitting through another one of Mr. Banks' lec-

* Augie Kunkel won first prize a year later.

tures. In desperation he shouted, "Mrs. Carillon!" at the top of his lungs.

Tony's piercing yell startled everyone at the table. Even Mrs. Carillon looked up as if aroused from a deep sleep.

"Yes, Tony?" she said.

Duck!

"Uh, Mrs. Carillon," Tony repeated in a lowered voice, red-faced over his unexpected outburst, "uh . . . you're not eating your duck."

"Duck?" she said, inspecting the piece on her plate. "Duck?" Mrs. Carillon looked around the table. For the first time since she learned the true meaning of the *glub-blubs,* Mrs. Carillon smiled.

"Remember the last time we had duck?" she said, ". . .and the lace underwear . . . and Augie's poor head. . . ." Mrs. Carillon couldn't continue; she was laughing too hard.

Mr. Banks thought he must be listening to the babblings of a lunatic.

Tina, Tony, and Augie Kunkel were laughing, too. They laughed at Mr. Banks' frightened face, and they laughed because Mrs. Carillon had "gotten over it." They laughed even louder when Augie Kunkel wiped his glasses with the greasy napkin and displayed his dirty spectacles; and when Mrs. Baker served the Camembert cheese, they laughed so hard they almost fell off their chairs.

Mr. Banks, realizing that all was well and back to its normal silliness, began eating again. He was the only one to have dessert; the others were too exhausted, and their cheeks hurt too much to eat.

Mrs. Carillon leaned back in her chair and returned the happy smiles that welcomed her back to reality.

"What day is today?" she asked.

"Tuesday, November 19," Augie Kunkel replied, wiping his glasses with a clean napkin. "It's almost Thanksgiving."

Mrs. Carillon paled. She brushed the back of her hand across her forehead and swept away the memory of an earlier turkey-less dinner.

"Let's really celebrate this year," she said, smiling again. "I have so much to be thankful for."

Turkey and Trimmings

The guests were expected at three o'clock. Mrs. Baker was chopping and mincing, grating and dicing, and singing away in a loud soprano. The twins were trying to figure out how many places to set at the table, but the noise from the kitchen made them lose count. They had never heard their cook sing before.

"She's happy because her sister is getting out of jail today," Tony explained.

"Then why is she singing 'I Love You Truly'?"

The doorbell rang between a "tru-" and an "ly," and in came Mr. Banks carrying a battered suitcase for a thin, smiling, gap-toothed woman. Spikes of red hair poked out from under her drooping hat. The frayed lining of her threadbare coat reached the heels of her shoes, which were so worn down on the sides she stood bowlegged.

"Tony, Tina, this is Mineola Potts," Mr. Banks said.

Mineola Potts smiled widely at the twins, revealing

even more toothless gaps; then she tiptoed across the room and peeked around the open kitchen door.

"Boo!" she said.

****

The twittering and giggling from the kitchen was even louder than the singing and chopping had been. Mr. Banks had to shout to make himself heard.

"Where's Mrs. Carillon? I've got a stack of bills here that will send us all to the poorhouse. She must have bought out every store in town."

"She's getting dressed," Tina said. "Besides, can't that wait until tomorrow? We're supposed to be celebrating."

"Help us count, Mr. Banks," Tony said, putting what he hoped was the last plate on the table.

"Don't they teach you anything in that school?" The words were the same, but Mr. Banks did not seem to be as grumpy as usual. "All right, I'll help you count. Tell me who's coming."

"Mrs. Carillon, Tina and me, and two of our friends, you and Mineola Potts, and Augie Kunkel and his Aunt Martha."

"That makes ten," Mr. Banks said.

"I counted nine."

"Ten," Mr. Banks insisted. "You forgot Mrs. Baker."

"Mrs. Baker? Then who's going to serve?"

"We can serve ourselves. Mrs. Baker has worked long and hard for you. She's as much a member of this family as anybody here."

"Why, Mr. Banks, that's socialism!"

"That's enough of your sass, young man. . . ."

Luckily for Tony, the doorbell rang.

****

"You must have the wrong apartment," Mr. Banks said curtly to the two young men at the door. One had long hair flowing from a beaded headband and a fringed beard that matched his fringed suede jacket. The other had a large puff of black hair and wore a serape and sandals.

"Harry! Joel!" Tina ran to the door. "These are our friends, Mr. Banks."

Mr. Banks was so dumbfounded that he was still holding the door open when Augie Kunkel and Aunt Martha arrived.

Aunt Martha was a short, hefty woman with close-cropped white hair. She, too, was wearing a fringed suede jacket.

"Glad to meet you," she said, grabbing Mr. Banks' hand and cracking every bone in his fingers.

The New Mrs. Carillon

Augie Kunkel introduced Aunt Martha to Tina, and Tina introduced everybody to everybody else. They all sat down, except Augie Kunkel, who stood in the center of the room waiting for Mrs. Carillon to appear. He was holding a bouquet of yellow roses.

"Yellow roses," remarked Mr. Banks. "I haven't seen anything but violets and purple anemones in this house since she moved in."

"Mrs. Carillon!" Tina gasped. Eyes popped and jaws dropped in amazement. A stunned silence greeted Mrs. Carillon as she circled the room welcoming her guests.

"It's so good to see you again, Joel. Harry," she said. "And you must be Aunt Martha."

Mrs. Carillon's hair was short and brown and softly

waved. She was wearing an elegantly tailored, beige wool dress, a string of pearls, and brown calf shoes.

"Augie, how thoughtful. Yellow roses, my favorite* flower."

"You look b-b-beautiful."

Mr. Banks thought so, too. "I must say, if that's what you spent all that money on, it was worth it."

"Mrs. Carillon!" Mineola Potts dashed out of the kitchen into the arms of her old cellmate.

"Dinner's ready," Mrs. Baker announced. She herded the guests to the lavishly spread table and took her seat among them.

Mr. Banks carved the turkey; the plates were passed and filled high to overflowing; and Mrs. Carillon asked Augie Kunkel to say grace.

Augie Kunkel didn't know how to say grace. He just named the dishes and let the delicious smells inspire the proper reverence:

> *Patate douce, dindonneau truffée,*
> *airelles en couronne, petits oignons,*
> *pointes d'asperges au beurre,*
> *purée de marrons.*

"Amen," said Mr. Banks, who didn't understand French; and the eating and the chatting and the celebrating began.

The Eating and the Chatting

Tina asked Mineola Potts to describe every horrible detail of her miserable life in the "pest-hole"; and Mrs. Car-

---

* True. She thought Noel was the one who liked purple.

illon told Aunt Martha how sorry she was that her house was falling down around her ears.

"Delicious," said Mr. Banks, tasting the turkey. Mrs. Baker beamed.

Aunt Martha replied that it was just awful, because now she would have to move in with Augie. "Not that I'm not fond of Augie, I am; but he doesn't have room for my work."

"Aunt Martha is an artist," Augie Kunkel explained.

"Delicious," said Mr. Banks, tasting the stuffing.

Joel said he understood Aunt Martha's problem very well, for they had just lost the lease to their loft and would soon be without a place to work, too.

"Rats as big as cats," Mineola Potts said to wide-eyed Tina.

"Do you paint in oils or watercolors?" Harry asked Aunt Martha, more in politeness than interest.

"Who do you think I am, Grandma Moses?" she replied. "Kinetic sculpture, that's what I do. You know, where everything moves. . . ."

"But the people were nice," Mineola Potts said. "That is, all but one. We avoided her like the plague. In for child-beating, she was; name of Anna Oglethorpe."

"Miss Anna Oglethorpe! In jail?" exclaimed Mrs. Carillon.

Mr. Banks looked up from his plate. "Not again?"

"No, not again," Mrs. Carillon had little sympathy for her former governess. "Miss Anna Oglethorpe can stay right where she is." *

"I had a show a few years back," Aunt Martha said,

---

* The pest-hole was finally closed down, and Miss Anna Oglethorpe was sent to a modern prison on Rikers Island, where she was very unhappy. She missed her pet rat.

"but, just my luck, it opened the very day of the black-out. No electricity. All my pieces are motor-driven, so nothing worked."

Mr. Banks said "delicious" five more times, while Joel, Harry, and Aunt Martha discussed techniques and consoled each other over their loss of working space.

"I have a wonderful idea," Mrs. Carillon said to the artists. "My big old house. There's plenty of living room and working room there for all of you. That is, if you don't mind overlooking a soup factory."

"Sounds great," Joel said, "but I don't think we could afford it."

"The house is a gift—to the three of you. It's little enough for what you did for the twins and me," Mrs. Carillon said to Joel and Harry, then turned to Aunt Martha, "and for all you've done for Augie. Mr. Banks, would you draw up the papers tomorrow?"

Tina and Tony cringed, expecting Mr. Banks to spoil the party with a loud "No!" They couldn't believe that he said, "Of course, fine idea." And he was smiling.

"Well, Miss Tinglehof, it seems we're partners," Harry said.

"Who's Miss Tinglehof?" Tina asked, looking around the table.

"That's me, Martha Tinglehof." Aunt Martha raised her glass of wine. "To Tietelbaum, Tinglehof, and Wells. That's alphabetical."

"Who's Tietelbaum? Who's Wells?"

"Harry Tietelbaum."

"Joel Wells."

The three artists clinked glasses.

"Artists?" Mr. Banks said. "You sound more like a law firm." He poured a little wine into the twins' glasses.

"Maybe that's what I'll be, a lawyer," Tony said, in appreciation of Mr. Banks' sudden good humor; but Tina still eyed his cheerfulness with suspicion.

The Celebrating

Mr. Banks returned to the head of the table and clinked a knife against his wineglass.

"As most of you know," he began when he had everyone's attention, "I have served Mrs. Carillon as trustee for many years, and, in return, was always warmly welcomed as a friend.

"Today, I am pleased to announce, I am here at this festive occasion, not only as trustee and friend, but as a proud and happy husband."

Tina slumped down in her chair. Tony bit his lip to keep from crying out. Augie Kunkel turned as white as the tablecloth had been before the wine stains and gravy spots.

"I know this comes as a surprise," Mr. Banks continued, "but since it is the second marriage for both of us, Bertha and I. . ."

"Bertha? Who's Bertha?" shouted Tina, Tony, and Mr. Kunkel at the same time.

"Why, Mrs. Baker, of course; I mean Mrs. Banks." Mr. Banks wondered what all the confusion was about. "As I was saying, Bertha and I went down to City Hall yesterday, and. . ."

"I don't think anyone is really interested in the details, Bertram," Mrs. Banks said to her new husband.

"Bertram?" laughed Tony.

****

Glasses were raised in a happy toast to the newlyweds. Tony offered them a gift of the remaining five months' supply of Camembert cheese, and Mr. Banks accepted. Augie Kunkel wiped the beads of perspiration from his brow and sighed a deep sigh of relief.

"Mr. Kunkel has something to say," Tina announced.

"Yes, Mr. Kunkel, go ahead," coaxed Tony. "Ask her!"

Everyone at the table—except Mr. and Mrs. Banks, who were staring into each other's eyes—noticed Augie Kunkel's embarrassment and understood what the twins wanted him to say.

"I d-d-don't think this is the p-p-proper t-t-time."

"Yes, it is, Augie," Mrs. Carillon said. "I think this is a lovely time."

Augie Kunkel blushed, rose from his chair, and raised the wineglass in his trembling hand. Tina closed her eyes and prayed he wouldn't stutter.

He didn't. He spoke slowly and gracefully.

"This is a joyous time for me, too; for I am with those who are dearest to me: my good Aunt Martha, my impatient friends Tina and Tony, and the beautiful Mrs. Carillon."

"Ask her, already," Tony urged.

Mr. Kunkel cleared his throat and began again.

"There is so much I would like to say, but I'm afraid the audience is getting restless. My dear Mrs. Carillon, I have little to offer but my constant devotion and undying. . ."

"Mr. Kunkel is asking you to marry him," Tina explained.

"Please, Mrs. Carillon, say 'Yes'!" Tony begged.

Mrs. Carillon looked up at her nervous suitor and smiled.

"Caroline Kunkel," she said. "What a lovely name."

A Happy Ending

Her name was now Caroline Fish Carillon Kunkel; but everyone still called her Mrs. Carillon, even Augie and the twins. The four of them spent a jolly honeymoon on the horse farm, while the apartment was redecorated in yellow and floor-to-ceiling bookcases were installed.

Tina and Tony adored Augie Kunkel who, to no one's surprise, proved a loving father and most devoted husband. Even after the twins had grown up and moved on, Mrs. Carillon and Augie Kunkel still thought of themselves as newlyweds. They lived long, and their late marriage lasted forty wonderful years.

****

Most of the people in our story lived to a ripe old age. Some achieved fame; others, love. One was hit by a truck and another disappeared; but when all is tallied and compared to real life, this is truly a happy ending.

****

Mr. and Mrs. Banks had little excitement in their lives, which was just the way they wanted it. They respected each other's good helping of common sense, and Mr. Banks grew fat on his wife's cooking. After her husband's death, Bertha Baker Banks wrote a cookbook with recipe names supplied by Augie Kunkel. It sold over one million copies.

****

Mineola Potts worked as cook in the Kunkel household (the job Mr. Banks had found for her). Her meals were mediocre, to say the least; but she entertained the family for hours on end with tales of her incredible adventures. One day, soon after the twins had left for college, the wanderlust returned. Minnie disappeared and was never heard from again.

****

Harry Tietelbaum gave up his art career to organize the successful Pomato Soup Workers' strike. He went on from there to clam chowder, black bean, and chicken noodle; but it was the alphabet soup sit-in that won him a name as a leading labor leader.

****

Aunt Martha Tinglehof had her one-man show at the age of ninety-three. Everything worked this time, and she sold several pieces of her kinetic sculpture.

****

Joel Wells worked long and hard at his art. Fame was slow in coming, but eventually museums began to buy his work, then private collectors; and finally the critics called him "America's Greatest Living Painter." Joel replied, "Grape," rebuilt the old house into studios, and set up a colony for struggling young artists.

****

Mavis Bensonhurst's mother suffered a broken arm when she was hit by a truck. She was wearing a pantsuit at the time, so no one saw her lace underwear. The driver claimed that his truck had stopped for a light and that

Mrs. Bensonhurst had slipped on some dog dung while crossing the street and dented his fender. The truck company sued Mrs. Bensonhurst for damages, and Mrs. Bensonhurst sued the poodle.

****

Tony Carillon had a happy life with his pretty wife Rosemary Neuberger and their triplets. He landed in the public's eye as a lawyer for the poodle in the Bensonhurst case. In later years, he proved a wise and honest judge, especially when there was a jury to make the decision.

****

Dr. Tina Carillon, the famous neurologist, was so busy with her research, her private practice, and her free clinic for orphans, that she never had the time or the desire to marry. Tina accomplished something quite rare in the annals of medicine: she not only discovered a new disease (Carillon's disease), but two years later found the cure for it.

****

Newton Pinckney never won an Oscar, but he had a long career as a character actor. He always played the villain.

****

Jordan Pinckney flunked out of Yale and became a used-car salesman in Hackensack, New Jersey.

****

All of our people were happy or famous, or both; except for Jordan Pinckney and Mrs. Bensonhurst (the poodle won). Perhaps the happiest were Mrs. Carillon, Augie Kunkel, and Tony. One might call Mrs. Bertha Baker Banks famous, certainly Tina and Joel; but the most famous of all was the one whose name was known throughout the world:

Christmas Bells, the horse who came from nowhere to outsprint the sprinters and outstay the stayers, became a legend. Sure with his mares, he sired a great line including the champions Yuletide, Sleigh Bells, and Ding Dong. Each was unbeatable at any distance, but none had the magic of Christmas Bells—the greatest horse of all time.

Ellen Raskin had three names. She wrote and illustrated many books under her first two names: Ellen Raskin. At other times she was known as Mrs. Flanagan because she was married to Dennis Flanagan, former editor of *Scientific American*, who dumped her out of a sailboat on their honeymoon.

Ellen Raskin was born in Milwaukee, Wisconsin, and grew up during the Great Depression. She is the author of several other novels, including the Newbery Award–winning *The Westing Game*, the Newbery Honor–winning *Figgs & Phantoms*, and *The Tattooed Potato and other clues*. She also wrote and illustrated many picture books, and was an accomplished graphic artist. She designed dust jackets for dozens of books, including the first edition of Madeleine L'Engle's classic *A Wrinkle in Time*. Ms. Raskin died at the age of fifty-six on August 8, 1984, in New York City.

The word-pictures were drawn and lettered by the author in pen and ink. The display type is Craw Clarendon Condensed, and the text type is Times Roman.

Turn the page
to read the first two chapters of Ellen Raskin's
Newbery Award–winning novel,

THE
WESTING
GAME

1

THE SUN SETS in the west (just about everyone knows that), but Sunset Towers faced east. Strange!

Sunset Towers faced east and had no towers. This glittery, glassy apartment house stood alone on the Lake Michigan shore five stories high. Five empty stories high.

Then one day (it happened to be the Fourth of July), a most uncommon-looking delivery boy rode around town slipping letters under the doors of the chosen tenants-to-be. The letters were signed *Barney Northrup*.

The delivery boy was sixty-two years old, and there was no such person as Barney Northrup.

■ ■ ■ ■ ■ ■ ■ ■ ■ ■ ■

Dear Lucky One:

Here it is—the apartment you've always dreamed of, at a
rent you can afford, in the newest, most luxurious building
on Lake Michigan:

SUNSET TOWERS

- Picture windows in every room
- Uniformed doorman, maid service
- Central air conditioning, hi-speed elevator
- Exclusive neighborhood, near excellent schools
- Etc., etc.

You have to see it to believe it. But these unbelievably elegant apartments will be shown by appointment only. So
hurry, there are only a few left!!! Call me now at 276-7474
for this once-in-a-lifetime offer.

Your servant,
Barney Northrup

P.S. I am also renting ideal space for:
- Doctor's office in lobby
- Coffee shop with entrance from parking lot
- Hi-class restaurant on entire top floor

■ ■ ■ ■ ■ ■ ■ ■ ■ ■ ■

Six letters were delivered, just six. Six appointments were made,
and one by one, family by family, talk, talk, talk, Barney Northrup led the tours around and about Sunset Towers.

"Take a look at all that glass. One-way glass," Barney Northrup said. "You can see out, nobody can see in."

Looking up, the Wexlers (the first appointment of the day)

were blinded by the blast of morning sun that flashed off the face of the building.

"See those chandeliers? Crystal!" Barney Northrup said, slicking his black moustache and straightening his hand-painted tie in the lobby's mirrored wall. "How about this carpeting? Three inches thick!"

"Gorgeous," Mrs. Wexler replied, clutching her husband's arm as her high heels wobbled in the deep plush pile. She, too, managed an approving glance in the mirror before the elevator door opened.

"You're really in luck," Barney Northrup said. "There's only one apartment left, but you'll love it. It was meant for you." He flung open the door to 3D. "Now, is that breathtaking, or is that breathtaking?"

Mrs. Wexler gasped; it was breathtaking, all right. Two walls of the living room were floor-to-ceiling glass. Following Barney Northrup's lead, she ooh-ed and aah-ed her joyous way through the entire apartment.

Her trailing husband was less enthusiastic. "What's this, a bedroom or a closet?" Jake Wexler asked, peering into the last room.

"It's a bedroom, of course," his wife replied.

"It looks like a closet."

"Oh Jake, this apartment is perfect for us, just perfect," Grace Wexler argued in a whining coo. The third bedroom was a trifle small, but it would do just fine for Turtle. "And think what it means having your office in the lobby, Jake; no more driving to and from work, no more mowing the lawn or shoveling snow."

"Let me remind you," Barney Northrup said, "the rent here is cheaper than what your old house costs in upkeep."

How would he know that, Jake wondered.

Grace stood before the front window where, beyond the road, beyond the trees, Lake Michigan lay calm and glistening. A lake view! Just wait until those so-called friends of hers with their classy houses see this place. The furniture would have to be reupholstered; no, she'd buy new furniture—beige velvet. And she'd have stationery made—blue with a deckle edge, her name and fancy address in swirling type across the top: *Grace Windsor Wexler, Sunset Towers on the Lake Shore.*

■ ■ ■ ■ ■ ■ ■ ■ ■ ■ ■

Not every tenant-to-be was quite as overjoyed as Grace Windsor Wexler. Arriving in the late afternoon, Sydelle Pulaski looked up and saw only the dim, warped reflections of treetops and drifting clouds in the glass face of Sunset Towers.

"You're really in luck," Barney Northrup said for the sixth and last time. "There's only one apartment left, but you'll love it. It was meant for you." He flung open the door to a one-bedroom apartment in the rear. "Now, is that breathtaking or is that breathtaking?"

"Not especially," Sydelle Pulaski replied as she blinked into the rays of the summer sun setting behind the parking lot. She had waited all these years for a place of her own, and here it was, in an elegant building where rich people lived. But she wanted a lake view.

"The front apartments are taken," Barney Northrup said. "Besides, the rent's too steep for a secretary's salary. Believe me, you get the same luxuries here at a third of the price."

At least the view from the side window was pleasant. "Are you sure nobody can see in?" Sydelle Pulaski asked.

"Absolutely," Barney Northrup said, following her suspicious stare to the mansion on the north cliff. "That's just the old Westing house up there; it hasn't been lived in for fifteen years."

"Well, I'll have to think it over."

"I have twenty people begging for this apartment," Barney Northrup said, lying through his buckteeth. "Take it or leave it."

"I'll take it."

Whoever, whatever else he was, Barney Northrup was a good salesman. In one day he had rented all of Sunset Towers to the people whose names were already printed on the mailboxes in an alcove off the lobby:

OFFICE	❏	*Dr. Wexler*
LOBBY	❏	*Theodorakis Coffee Shop*
2C	❏	*F. Baumbach*
2D	❏	*Theodorakis*
3C	❏	*S. Pulaski*
3D	❏	*Wexler*
4C	❏	*Hoo*
4D	❏	*J. J. Ford*
5	❏	*Shin Hoo's Restaurant*

Who were these people, these specially selected tenants? They were mothers and fathers and children. A dressmaker, a secretary, an inventor, a doctor, a judge. And, oh yes, one was a bookie, one was a burglar, one was a bomber, and one was a mistake. Barney Northrup had rented one of the apartments to the wrong person.

■ GHOSTS OR WORSE ■

2 ON SEPTEMBER FIRST, the chosen ones (and the mistake) moved in. A wire fence had been erected along the north side of the building; on it a sign warned:

NO TRESPASSING—*Property of the Westing estate.*

The newly paved driveway curved sharply and doubled back on itself rather than breach the city-county line. Sunset Towers stood at the far edge of town.

On September second, Shin Hoo's Restaurant, specializing in authentic Chinese cuisine, held its grand opening. Only three people came. It was, indeed, an exclusive neighborhood; too exclusive for Mr. Hoo. However, the less expensive coffee shop that opened on the parking lot was kept busy serving breakfast, lunch, and dinner to tenants "ordering up" and to workers from nearby Westingtown.

Sunset Towers was a quiet, well-run building, and (except for the grumbling Mr. Hoo) the people who lived there seemed content. Neighbor greeted neighbor with "Good morning" or "Good evening" or a friendly smile, and grappled with small problems behind closed doors.

The big problems were yet to come.

■ ■ ■ ■ ■ ■ ■ ■ ■ ■ ■

Now it was the end of October. A cold, raw wind whipped dead leaves about the ankles of the four people grouped in the Sunset Towers driveway, but not one of them shivered. Not yet.

The stocky, broad-shouldered man in the doorman's uniform, standing with feet spread, fists on hips, was Sandy McSouthers. The two slim, trim high-school seniors, shielding their eyes against the stinging chill, were Theo Theodorakis and Doug Hoo. The small, wiry man pointing to the house on the hill was Otis Amber, the sixty-two-year-old delivery boy.

They faced north, gaping like statues cast in the moment of discovery, until Turtle Wexler, her kite tail of a braid flying behind her, raced her bicycle into the driveway. "Look! Look, there's smoke—there's smoke coming from the chimney of the Westing house."

The others had seen it. What did she think they were looking at anyway?

Turtle leaned on the handlebars, panting for breath. (Sunset Towers was near excellent schools, as Barney Northrup had promised, but the junior high was four miles away.) "Do you think—do you think old man Westing's up there?"

"Naw," Otis Amber, the old delivery boy, answered. "Nobody's seen him for years. Supposed to be living on a private island in the South Seas, he is; but most folks say he's dead.

Long-gone dead. They say his corpse is still up there in that big old house. They say his body is sprawled out on a fancy Oriental rug, and his flesh is rotting off those mean bones, and maggots are creeping in his eye sockets and crawling out his nose holes." The delivery boy added a high-pitched he-he-he to the gruesome details.

Now someone shivered. It was Turtle.

"Serves him right," Sandy said. At other times a cheery fellow, the doorman often complained bitterly about having been fired from his job of twenty years in the Westing paper mill. "But somebody must be up there. Somebody alive, that is." He pushed back the gold-braided cap and squinted at the house through his steel-framed glasses as if expecting the curling smoke to write the answer in the autumn air. "Maybe it's those kids again. No, it couldn't be."

"What kids?" the three kids wanted to know.

"Why, those two unfortunate fellas from Westingtown."

"What unfortunate fellas?" The three heads twisted from the doorman to the delivery boy. Doug Hoo ducked Turtle's whizzing braid. Touch her precious pigtail, even by accident, and she'll kick you in the shins, the brat. He couldn't chance an injury to his legs, not with the big meet coming. The track star began to jog in place.

"Horrible, it was horrible," Otis Amber said with a shudder that sent the loose straps of his leather aviator's helmet swinging about his long, thin face. "Come to think of it, it happened exactly one year ago tonight. On Halloween."

"What happened?" Theo Theodorakis asked impatiently. He was late for work in the coffee shop.

"Tell them, Otis," Sandy urged.

The delivery boy stroked the gray stubble on his pointed chin. "Seems it all started with a bet; somebody bet them a dollar they couldn't stay in that spooky house five minutes. One measly buck! The poor kids hardly got through those French doors on this side of the Westing house when they came tearing out like they was being chased by a ghost. Chased by a ghost—or worse."

Or worse? Turtle forgot her throbbing toothache. Theo Theodorakis and Doug Hoo, older and more worldly-wise, exchanged winks but stayed to hear the rest of the story.

"One fella ran out crazy-like, screaming his head off. He never stopped screaming 'til he hit the rocks at the bottom of the cliff. The other fella hasn't said but two words since. Something about purple."

Sandy helped him out. "Purple waves."

Otis Amber nodded sadly. "Yep, that poor fella just sits in the state asylum saying, 'Purple waves, purple waves' over and over again, and his scared eyes keep staring at his hands. You see, when he came running out of the Westing house, his hands was dripping with warm, red blood."

Now all three shivered.

"Poor kid," the doorman said. "All that pain and suffering for a dollar bet."

"Make it two dollars for each minute I stay in there, and you're on," Turtle said.

■ ■ ■ ■ ■ ■ ■ ■ ■ ■ ■

Someone was spying on the group in the driveway.

From the front window of apartment 2D, fifteen-year-old Chris Theodorakis watched his brother Theo shake hands (it must be a bet) with the skinny, one-pigtailed girl and rush into the lobby. The family coffee shop would be busy now; his brother should have been working the counter half an hour ago. Chris checked the wall clock. Two more hours before Theo would bring up his dinner. Then he would tell him about the limper.

Earlier that afternoon Chris had followed the flight of a purple martin (*Progne subis*) across the field of brambles, through the oaks, up to the red maple on the hill. The bird flew off, but something else caught his eye. Someone (he could not tell if the person was a man or a woman) came out of the shadows on the lawn, unlocked the French doors, and disappeared into the Westing house. Someone with a limp. Minutes later smoke began to rise from the chimney.

Once again Chris turned toward the side window and scanned the house on the cliff. The French doors were closed; heavy drapes hung full against the seventeen windows he had counted so many times.

They didn't need drapes on the special glass windows here in Sunset Towers. He could see out, but nobody could see in. Then why did he sometimes feel that someone was watching him? Who could be watching him? God? If God was watching, then why was he like this?

The binoculars fell to the boy's lap. His head jerked, his body coiled, lashed by violent spasms. Relax, Theo will come soon. Relax, soon the geese will be flying south in a V. Canada goose (*Branta canadensis*). Relax. Relax and watch the wind tangle the smoke and blow it toward Westingtown.

Don't miss any of Ellen Raskin's clever mysteries!

Hardcover 978-0-525-42369-0
Paperback 978-0-14-241700-3

Hardcover 978-0-525-42367-6
Paperback 978-0-14-241169-8

Hardcover 978-0-525-42368-3
Paperback 978-0-14-241699-0

Dutton 25th Anniversary Edition
978-0-525-47137-0

Puffin Premium Edition
978-0-14-038664-6

Puffin Modern Classics Edition
978-0-14-240120-0